OPERATION
SAVING THE GIFT

Michael Colon

2026, TWB Press
www.twbpress.com

Operation Saving the Gift

Edited by Terry Wright

Cover Art by Terry Wright

ISBN: 978-1-967888-12-2

Chapter 1

The view from above the clouds never gets old. The amount of time I spend in the sky during my travels has been just as good as the lands I get to explore. The blue world is my place of refuge, and I intend to see parts of the world I am still learning about. I've only scratched the surface of what's out there. The lands I've already explored did not have humans or codexes. It still seems like my country is the only place that has civilization. I have an explorer's heart and would love to see other countries with civilizations on the rise. The world can finally be what it once was.

I write in my travel journal that has sketches and descriptions of the experiences I've had during my expeditions. During this one, I got to visit various mountainous regions and climb up to the peaks. I rub my hand over those sketches of the views I saw from the mountain tops and long to go back to see more as soon as I can. That won't be easy because of how strict my commander is toward me.

I set a course for home in the GPS system and put my plane on autopilot. I lean back in my seat and look up at the different shapes of clouds. Staring into the atmosphere, I think about the place called Heaven. I wonder if Aelius and his parents are at that place. Joseph told me that Heaven exists outside the rules of this life. That the afterlife is located in a place that our minds can't fully comprehend. That in Heaven we are in a state God created us to be in, and anything is possible. The plane shakes from turbulence. I jump forward and grab the wheel to regain control of my aircraft, but the autopilot holds true. I chuckle thinking about the first time that happened to me and how much I panicked.

A flock of birds glide beside the wings of my plane. I wave to the birds, and they all disperse into the milky sky. Atlandia, which I call home, reveals itself below as the thin layer of clouds fades.

I descend to my country and land on the coastline of New Haven in all its beauty. The shining star of Atlandia. We were the first Haven to come into existence on the continent, back when we referred to ourselves as Old Haven. I jump out of the cockpit and take my most precious item from the back seat. I kiss the photo of Aelius and his family and put it in my pocket.

As I walk along the shoreline, I think about how grateful I am for his friendship. All these years later, I have never forgotten all the memories we made together. And I never will. A big smile grows across my face. I know how the world has changed for the better ever since we received his gift thirty-some years ago. When I was a little girl, this beach was forbidden to walk along because of the threat from codex units. Now they help us keep it clean.

I approach the tall, heavily reinforced iron gates and knock hard. Security confirms my identity, and then the gates unlock and open. I take my first couple steps into New Haven.

The guards salute me. "Captain, it's so good to see you."

"It's good to be home. I missed you guys. How has it been here?"

"Nothing we couldn't handle. Failed attempts of breach by a few small groups of Zeros here and there." The Zeros are groups of people who don't believe in the new ways of history and would rather abide by the old ways. After we received the gift, many people remained outside the Havens, and over the decades, their numbers increased, as did their radicalized ideologies, although, for whatever reason, they think the same of us.

I give the New Haven salute to the guards and walk throughout town. The world has changed so much over the years. Now there are twelve strong Havens in Atlandia that are becoming like small cities.

The United Havens of Atlandia is the only continent that has sophisticated civilizations in the world. We are connected by a railroad system that goes throughout the country. These railroads were built right after Joseph passed away, but he left us the blueprints to build them. The railroads are lifelines for us and the other Havens so we can stay connected and help each other. The first pioneers of Old Haven made their pilgrimage in every direction of the country to start their own Havens. Because mankind and codex built these railroads soon after The Great Unison, all the Havens worked together and still do for the betterment of this new history. The Great Unison is when man and codex officially stopped fighting each other.

During the Great Unison, the twelve havens were constructed, and a peace treaty was formed with constitutional laws. Codex units are now classified as law-abiding civilians with basic human rights. The only way the world gets back to how it used to be is to let go of the hatred we had and pave a new way. But these Zeros refuse to claim citizenship into one of the twelve, and thus they make things complicated. We gave them this name because they choose to remain a primitive faction who are against this new world of progress. The Zeros are a bunch of savages.

A class of kids and codexes run over to me with

gifts. Debra follows behind them with a smile on her face. The class hands me necklaces made of seashells. I had asked them to make these for me before my first trip. They bombard me with questions.

Debra tells her class, "Okay everyone, give Lucy some room to breathe." Debrah is a teacher for a school in New Haven. She specializes in history and literature. She does parttime nursing, too. Debra made it her life's goal to help the next generation coming up to be better citizens and build upon this beautiful country. "How was your adventure?"

"I enjoyed it very much. But there is so much more to explore. I am glad to be back home for now."

Debrah comes close and gives me a kiss on the forehead. "You are like a daughter to me. I am so proud of not just the soldier you are, but the woman you grew to be. Joseph would be so proud of you."

I put on the seashell necklace made by her class. It is beautiful, made of different colored shells and rocks.

One of the students ask me, "Did you have to kill enemies in the foreign places you went to?"

"No. I did not see any enemies to our home in far away places. Our home is safe."

Another student asks, "I heard that you're one of the best soldiers. Is it true that you took out four Zeros by yourself with just a knife?"

Debra tells her class, "It's time to head back to school now. Recess is over. We will talk to Lucy soon."

I wave goodbye to them and watch Debra escort her class back. She winks at me. I walk around New Haven past the floral shops, market places, recreational areas, and people's homes.

Some laborers who are building a couple new homes all acknowledge and welcome me home. A lead architect asks, "If it isn't the star with wings herself. How was your trip?"

"It was amazing, Ronaldo. But now duty calls."

"Yeah. Trust me. I get it. I know you're not allowed to say this, but tell Blackwater to get the stick out of his rear-end."

"The story of my life, Ronaldo."

Him saying that brings back memories to when I first started my military duty. He and our Elder never got along and butted heads about how we should approach our standard procedures and how we interact with the other Havens. General Teddy Blackwater is the head of the New Haven department of security forces. He became the general of our army because the former General was assassinated by a codex unit around the end of the Old Ways. Most people think that Teddy was moved up to the general rank too quickly because there were other veterans who could have held that title more honorably. Then again, Teddy probably thinks the same way about me being a captain and not a cadet anymore.

I stop by the New Haven Botanical Garden and sit down on a bench facing a tribute statue of Elder Joseph and Aelius. They were the most influential human and codex of our country at the time. Parents with their kids enjoy this beautiful day in the garden as they laugh and scream with joy. What a nice sight. Those children will see a better world and so will their children. Just like Joseph, who was like a grandfather to me, I enjoy sitting in the garden to decompress and think. Usually after a long day of duties. Before Joseph passed away, he kept telling me how nature represents the simple yet powerful force of life. No matter what life grows toward the light and flourishes. Life always wins. And I, as a skilled captain, will always fight for the side of a better life.

After giving myself the grace of peace I needed, I get up and leave the garden to go to the top of the border wall. Only a few people have authorization to go up there. Since I am still active in the military, I can come up here freely. I salute the guards and tell them why I am here. I sit down with my legs dangling off the ledge of the wall. Just like being in the clouds, this view will never get old.

"My Lucy has come home," Elder Michael says.

I get up and give him a big hug.

He chuckles. "Remember, I am an old man now. I know you can handle yourself, captain. I am glad you are safe and back home."

"I missed you, Michael. Thank you for approving my trip. My superiors kept denying my request until you overruled their commands. I know they may be upset at me, but I needed to keep my promise to Aelius."

Michael became Elder soon after Joseph died, and then he transformed Old Haven into New Haven. Michael took the reins from Joseph and honored his legacy by being a father-like figure to all the citizens here. He is not supposed to show favoritism as our leader, but he always makes sure I am taken care of first. I am like a daughter to him. Some of the military forces notice this love we have and can be jerks toward me for that, including the general. It's not my fault Michael and the runners all those years back found me starving to death in the wilderness.

When I was a little girl separated from my parents, I had to travel with a group to survive. The people of that group often would mistreat me. One day they left me for dead because they thought if I can't carry my own weight I would cost them their lives during the extermination by codexes. Some nights I have nightmares about being abandoned like that.

Michael orders his personal guards to give us some space for a few minutes and sits on the ledge next to me. From up here, the lush wilderness we oversee seems like it goes on forever. The city's walls are taller than the tallest buildings. We don't have skyscrapers from long ago, but I am proud that New Haven strives to bring back the architecture from metropolises of the past. Brick by brick we are constructing the world the way our ancestors remember it.

"What's on your mind, Lucy? I know that pondering face so well."

"I have been having dreams lately that keep me up. I'll get a handle on them, and I'll be ready for my duties."

"You are a phenomenal soldier. I am so proud of you. But first, you are like a daughter to me. Come to me with anything that is bothering you."

I lean my head on Michael's shoulder.

My wireless radio receives an alert: *"Report to base."*

I give Michael a hug and leave the top of the border wall. I walk by a group of codex units and kids kicking a ball amongst each other. It's nice seeing them play a friendly game. As a soldier who is always ready for my duties, it's good to see this. It shows growth and progress with the world, and that what I fight for means something. At the town square's water fountain, I see Hannah sitting near it, studying.

The minute she sees me, she drops the book and runs over to me. "Lucy. I know you're very busy. But I want to hear all about your adventure."

"I will make time to hangout with you soon. The commander needs me at base. It's probably going to be a long day."

"I understand, Lucy. I still want you to train me in your cool combat skills so I can have a head start to be an awesome soldier like yourself."

I give Hannah a hug, and we do the New Haven salute. "One of these days, Hannah. Don't go trying to sneak out again, and I will consider it more."

Hannah is Michael's teenage daughter. They want her to be the next Elder. But she wants to be a soldier like me.

At the military base, all the soldiers from each regiment stand in single file lines at attention as General Teddy Blackwater stands in front of us at the main hanger. We all salute at the same time, and go back to standing straight with our wrists crossed behind our backs.

"Attention soldiers of New Haven Property. I have received multiple reports from our departments that show good standing with our services. Great work. But like always, there is more work to be done to make sure our Haven is a shining representation of the country. Our flag's logo of one bright star with wings is who we are and what we fight for. All your updated task sheets are at your stations. All of you are dismissed."

A higher-ranking officer tells me that Blackwater does not want me to leave yet.

I look up at the general as he twirls his revolver while staring at me with a distasteful scowl.

Teddy can be a real prick, and the only reason why he sounded so honorable in front of us is because today we are being examined by a few of Haven's judges and recorders. We do the same for other Havens to keep each other accountable for the sake of Atlandia's success as a nation.

I remain at attention as he walks next to me, spinning his gun on his fingers. "Lucy, how was your trip? Michael came through for you again, it seems."

Teddy was the first person to deny my request for leave by persuading the other senior officers and chiefs to not sign off on it.

"My trip was good, sir."

He continues walking around me, spinning his revolver. He is trying to intimidate me, but it's not working. "That's good. As long as you remember what side you're on. I know that Elder Michael intervened and reversed my orders last time. Just know that it won't happen again, because I will bring a case to the high court of judges who will never allow it. You are dismissed. Now get to your tasks. Now."

I salute and march away, angry at him for his comment. He is correct by saying he can start appealing Michael's decisions. The way Atlandia is structured as a fair-based system, the Elders don't have absolute control of everything going on in the nation. The twelve elders are the faces and moral leaders of their respective homes. They have oversight on how their Haven is run. Each department of operations that helps keep a Haven sustainable must operate under the rules of the Elder. But the leader of the Havens' forces has more liberties and leeway to make decisions for what they think is best for the safety of people and property. In a way, a military commander has close to the same authority as an Elder. Then we have judges who are a board of people who have equal authority of elders by settling matters of politics, laws, and other essential conflicts for the country.

While retrieving my task sheet of updated orders, I notice some soldiers talking about me and how I rather travel the world then stay here as a loyal servant of New Haven. I try to ignore them while reading my work sheet. I walk past them, and they all stare at me.

"Is there an issue?" I ask them.

One soldier says, "I hear you're one of the more talented soldiers on the force. You also left our home for a while. Some may question your allegiance."

Blackwater must have gotten in their heads, but questioning my loyalty is disrespectful. "The only thing that's keeping me from knocking you out is—"

"Go ahead. The Elder will play favoritism, and you won't get in trouble, so give it your best shot."

I roll my eyes and start my tasks. Even though the rookie soldiers already organized and cleaned the inventory room, I still have to reorganize everything. Teddy Blackwater gave me this task to be spiteful. I stare at the tall racks of weapons in this industrial warehouse space and exhale. After moving everything around and reorganizing the weapons, I go to the track and field where new recruits are running laps. There is a stack of heavy construction materials that I have to move to the other side of the base. Watching the new recruits run reminds me of when I first started going through this part of basic training and how rigorous it was on my body. I see myself younger, running with these rookies, but then I look at the piles of blocks and construction materials, I come back to reality.

I make at least thirty trips from end to end of the

base, and I'm drenched in sweat. One of the rookie cadets comes over to me and gives me a towel.

We salute.

"Honor to meet you, captain. I hope to be a skilled pilot and fighter like you one day."

"Just be the best version of yourself, rookie."

He runs back to his command to finish his drills.

Next, I go to relieve some guards at the southwest wall so they can rest and get something to eat. They salute and march off. Standing guard, I make sure my rifle is ready to be used at any moment. I look at the guards at another entry point. Their weapons are not ready to be used, and they're not paying attention to their surroundings. Of course, TJ is with that group. I can't abandon my post, but they are being reckless. They are taking shots into the wilderness, making a game out of who can hit the farthest object. I get it, being on border watch can be redundant, but still, I abandon my post and jog over to the unit.

"Guys. What you're doing is reckless. You all need to stop. It's a waste of ammo and can blow your cover." I give TJ a look like he should know better. I hear shrieks that a Zero makes coming from my post, and I run back to see a Zero trying to climb up the wall. I grab him and slam him to the ground then point my assault rifle at him. "Get away from here."

The Zero runs off, shrieking.

One of the higher-ranking chiefs at another part of the border wall rushes away. I know I'm going to hear about this sooner than later. I continue to relieve my guards instead of taking time to be a part of a meeting with the other higher-ranking officers. One of them comes over to me and tells me to report back to base. "The general wants to see you."

I march into Blackwater's office. I see his revolver on the desk in front of him.

He looks up at me. "So, I heard you abandoned your post when relieving Carlos and Michah. As a captain, you should be the one setting the example."

"Yes. I agree. But there were privates acting irresponsibly. So I went to correct them before something bad happened to them."

"You still could have handled that situation much better. And you know this too. For that. I am assigning you to do exterior patrols around the entire perimeter of New Haven and our property outside the walls. I expect a full and detailed report right after you're done working at midnight."

"Tonight? I've been working all day, sir."

"You'll pull a double shift. You are dismissed."

"Yes, sir." I salute and march out of his office. In the courtyard, I sit on the bleacher seats, watching the new cadets do their marching drills. I ball up my fists, thinking about Teddy being unfair to me. Even through basic training, he always made me do much more and wouldn't reward me. Me being the first female officer upsets him. But regardless of gender, I am still a warrior for our country, and a good one, at that.

Before starting my endless rounds of perimeter patrols, I leave the empty courtyard while the guards on base go home. The sun is setting, and I see myself in my training outfit doing pushups. Way more push ups than the men. Teddy still has the nerve to judge me for being a woman. I can handle myself so much better than all the officers. I look behind me and see a time when I had to learn close-quarters combat. I was a natural at that, right away. All the cadets they paired with me to spar, I handled easily.

I start my patrol and walk miles around the perimeter until midnight when I can finally stop. I walk back to base with my feet burning and file my report, including time stamps. He will know if I did this task or not because of what the night watch reports.

I leave the military base to go back to my home. I soak in a bath, watching the soap bubbles pop. I think about that traumatic moment of waking up at camp with the group of survivors who took me in, only to abandon me for dead. I fully submerge myself in the bath water and close my eyes. I can hear my heartbeat, and in each beat, I hear Aelius and the conversations we had. I clutch the sides of the bathtub and continue to hold my breath. Now I find vague memories of a mother and father reaching out to me. A mother and father who died during the extermination process. I burst out of the bath water and scream.

I lie down in bed and stare up at the ceiling, thinking about the boatload of work I still need to do tomorrow, thanks to the honorable Blackwater. I finally feel tired and close my eyes, but when I open them I am in a jungle. Anxiety and terror consume me. I am a little girl again. Alone. I curl into a fetal position and cry. I hear a whisper call my name, and when I open my eyes, I am now in a city of sandy ruins. A codex unit hobbles in the distance. As I get closer to the codex, a sandstorm blows in. A gust of wind causes sand to blast me in the face, and I fall backwards. Before I can get up, the codex holds me down and leans in to get a closer look at me.

I wake up, screaming. I need to get up in a few hours, so I may as well get out of bed and get ready for the long day. I gear up in my tactical outfit and go to the beach to watch the sunrise, which is what I usually do before a long day. I keep thinking about the nightmare I had, so I take deep breaths while holding my photograph of Aelius close to my heart. I need to get it together. I am Lucy, captain and team leader in the New Haven Force.

"Well, well. Captain Lucy," a familiar voice says beside me. "I'm glad I found you to join me in watching a beautiful sunrise before our general keeps you away from me for another week of duties."

"How are you feeling, Lewis?" I hug him. "Has the medicine been helping you?"

Lewis adjusts his cane and faces the sunrise reflecting off the ocean. "I'm just an old man now. The medicine helps. But medicines can't heal everything. I keep my hope in the creator of mankind, that He will keep me alive."

Lewis has become a very empathetic person compared to when he, Michael, and the other runners first rescued me. Lewis used to be very bitter about losing his kids in the Old Times. He has had health issues recently, with his joints. His back and knees are constantly flaring up. He put his body through so much stress, but still holds the record for the number of runs in and out of Haven territory, before the New Haven Force was assembled. Now he is a counselor for citizens and military personnel.

"Can you believe it has been a little over thirty-three years since the world hit its pivotal turning point because of Aelius? I remember when we couldn't separate you two from wanting to play together."

"He was my best friend. I kept the photograph he gave me." I give it to Lewis.

He can't stop laughing. "Gosh. You really did take care of this photo. Who would have thought he once was this little boy? Holding this brings me back to when I was ready to shoot him that day in the parking lot. Am I glad I didn't do that all those years ago."

I take the photo back. "The world has been united ever since the Great Unison. Besides the Zeros who try to mess things up, and the political obstacles the havens ended up coming to agreements with, this has been the closest we've come to the world our ancestors lived in."

"Our ancestors didn't live in a perfect world, Lucy. People my age are like our ancestors, from back in the time of utopias. But I would like to see it that way again, at full capacity."

I hug Lewis and leave the beach and turn back to see him watching the sunrise. I get emotional seeing him standing there alone, knowing everything he has been through. But I need to get myself together for my duties on base. At my station, I sort through stacks of documents and reports that need to be reread and placed in the appropriate file cabinets for further action. Every time I finish a stack of paper work, a cadet comes over with a new stack, telling me, "Per request from the general." My body is still sore from the double shift of patrols, I barely got any sleep, and now I am back at it. This has been going on since Blackwater got promoted to general.

After multitasking through my shift, I sit down and take out my travel journal. This notebook has the dates and places I have seen on my previous adventure. I want my journal to be filled with as much information as possible before I die. There is so much more to see in this world. Who knows what else is out there that we can keep for making our country better. I jot down more coordinates for my next adventure, places I hope to visit. Chances are Teddy will deny my request and overrule Michael's approval. There are other continents that people of this nation haven't been to for many generations. There was a time when people would visit other corners of the planet, depending on the occasions and the availability of conventional means of public transportation. My ancestors used to take these getaways, called vacations, to bond with each other in a fun and carefree fashion. It would be amazing for us to get back to doing that one day. People used to take rockets into outer space, too...

I receive a code red on my radio, which means for me to report for an emergency dispatch mission.

Upon my arrival, I stand with a platoon of six including TJ, unfortunately. Hopefully he behaves on the mission and doesn't act irrational. TJ, ironically the youngest soldier here, is known for disobeying orders in the field and doing what he sees is right. Which usually is not the right choice.

General Blackwater approaches us, spinning his revolver. "You guys have been chosen to set out to save one of our codex civilians who is held hostage at a camp of Zeros. We finally have intel on where to retrieve him. Bring back our New Havener to his family."

We all salute and gather what we need for the mission, including weapons from the armory. While packing some ammunition, TJ walks by and bumps my shoulder on purpose. I almost drop the box of ammunition. I roll my eyes and give a long sigh.

While walking through the wilderness, TJ is bragging to the others in our platoon about his stat records during basic training. The only time I spoke was not to brag, but to give instructions as the team leader. The records that are set during the vetting process count, but the good work as a soldier is far more important. We exit the dense forest and enter a valley that does not provide much cover. While in our tactical formation, scanning the area, we see a few rocks fall from atop the canyon wall. We all draw our weapons at the same time.

"Everyone, stand by."

TJ says, "We need to go up there and handle those Zeros now."

"No. Hold your positions."

TJ darts up the valley canyon wall alone, disobeying my orders. Three of my guys go up the canyon to provide cover for him. Now it's just me and one troop.

"Don't move," a Zero says, pointing a pistol at me.

This guy came from a blind spot while I was focused on where the others went; and this troop near me is on his first mission. Normally we would scan the direction I was not looking, like covering each other's blind spots.

This Zero holds me at gunpoint, confounding my partner who is without fighting experience. A few more Zeros come down from the canyon with spears and blades to the necks of TJ and the soldiers I'd sent to cover him. That figures. They all go rushing to be heroes, and now they are held hostage.

Using my quick reflexes, I grab the pistol from the Zero because he doesn't have a proper handle on the gun. Now I hold him hostage at gunpoint. I motion the new recruit to stand a safe distance away, then tell the Zeros, "We don't want a blood bath. We are looking for someone to bring back home."

I know it's pointless to negotiate with the Zeros. They act like savages toward one another. I will commit murder if need be. Murder inside any haven is forbidden, other than in situations of self defense. The penalty is banishment. If I have to kill to defend New Haven, I will. It's times like these that I wish codexes could join the military. Our missions would go much smoother. A codex unit isn't impulsive and irrational. According to the law that Michael was the front runner on getting approved, and because of the life codexes had to live before, no codex will purposely be used as a tool for combat, unless absolutely necessary. Codex units are strictly given jobs that benefit society.

The savages across from me don't have any guns, but they press their sharp spears and blades on the necks of my comrades. Feeling the weight of this gun in my hands, I realize it has no bullets. It was just for show as a threat. I need to do something right now. No more wasting time.

I push my hostage a few feet in front of me, and within a heartbeat, I draw my sidearm and shoot around my Zero captive. He stumbles forward in front of me and falls, but I manage to hit a few Zeros. They run away because they have no defense against my gun. We let them go because our rules of engagement don't allow us to shoot them in the back. The rules state that we cannot execute a foreign or domestic threat that doesn't pose any level of significant threat to New Haven persons or property. Also, based on Michael's philosophy, how will we ever get back to the world as it used to be if we repeat the ways of the past, back when we were starving and struggling to survive.

I understand why we have rules of engagement. If we didn't, we wouldn't be any different from the Zeros. Society in Atlandia needs to be civil as we fight for our beliefs and freedoms. I pick up the Zero who had fallen and was left behind, and I demand for him to take us to our missing codex. I slap the Zero to snap him out of the shock he is in, and then I show him a picture of the codex civilian we are looking for.

"Okay. Okay. Don't shoot. I'll show you."

While pressing the barrel of my pistol on his head, he guides us out of the canyon and back into the forest. I order my team to get back into tactical formation since the fight may not be over yet. We get to an area where there is a group of Zeros around a campfire. Our codex civilian is tied up in cords. We fire our guns into the air, and they all run away. One that I wounded earlier hobbles off. We pull the codex to his feet, and my team unties him. I hug our codex member who is traumatized by the circumstances.

Codex units have feelings and can experience intense emotions like we do. Although they are geared more toward logic, they can experience trauma that can affect their personalities. I place my hand on top of our comrade's head and provide positive morale. Codex K5K1 tells us that they would not let him go until he gave information on how to get past our forces to invade our home. K5K1 never gave up any of our vulnerabilities to those monsters, even when they beat him.

"You are brave and strong," I tell him. "This is our fault that they snagged you, but we will make it up to you somehow."

We make our way back to New Haven. As soon as we get to our territory safe zone in the forest, I grab TJ and slam him against a tree. "Do you have any idea the danger you put us in because you decided to be an idiot?"

"I was making the best move for the team."

"You almost got everyone killed."

Everyone gets between us, and I let go of TJ.

TJ says, "The only reason you're team leader is because Michael loves his little orphan princess."

Without hesitating, I shove him backwards. He trips over his own feet and falls to the ground. Codex K1K5 guides me away, and the troops intervene to calm TJ down.

What a jerk for saying something like that. If it weren't for the codex, I would have given him a good butt kicking. He needs it badly.

As soon as the gates open, I go to the base and file my report about the mission without talking to anyone. At any moment, I expect to have a word with general jerk off, and right on time, I get a message to report to see him...asap. Me and TJ stand next to each other, facing General Blackwater.

"I hear that both of you got into a skirmish during the mission."

TJ marches two steps forward. "I made a judgment call for the betterment of the team. After retrieving our civilian, captain Lucy put her hands on me for her different view on the tactical move I made. There are better ways to handle these kinds of things...ah...sir." TJ never speaks this professionally.

I march three steps forward and before I state my case General Blackwater hands down his punishment. "Lucy. If something like this happens again, I will demote you to cadet. As punishment for your unprofessional actions, you are to finish the remaining reports assigned to TJ. And before you leave my sight, apologize to him right now."

I cannot believe this. I couldn't even get a single word out. Talk about feeling disrespected. I turn to TJ.

He smirks at me.

I want to punch him in the face, but I swallow my pride and give him the New Haven Salute. "Sorry I pushed you." I salute my general and immediately leave to do the extra tasks, which will take my mind off what happened. When I finish, I go to my house. To keep my moves sharp, I hit a heavy bag that is bolted to the ceiling, and with every blow, I think about how I am treated by the force.

I hear a knock on the door. It's Hannah.

"I didn't mean to disturb you, Lucy, but I would like to know if you can train me for a little while."

I bring Hannah inside and show her some basic strikes and how to keep distance. I can see that this makes her feel good. Her technique needs a lot of sharpening, but I know more importantly she appreciates this bonding time. Hannah is like a younger sister I never had.

"I want to be a strong soldier like you. Can you test my skills, me against you?"

"One day we can, Hannah. Hopefully by the time you're my age, there won't be a need for soldiers. I don't want to hurt you."

"Please. Please. Test me now but go easy on me."

I move some furniture out of the way and tell her to square her shoulders. "If you can land one clean shot on me I will buy you anything you want."

She lunges forward, trying to get a hit on me.

I weave out of all attempted strikes. After this goes on for another few minutes, she gets tired and sits on the floor. "You're too good, Lucy. I have a long way to go."

I sit on the floor next to her. "Let's get us a treat anyway, okay?"

I take Hannah's hand and lead her to the Haven's central square. We go to the vendor and ask for two ice creams. These types of foods are a rare treat. We walk around to see some public entertainment, which is people dancing in unusual ways by contorting their bodies.

"Hannah. Why do you want to join the force?"

"Because I. Well. Actually, I don't have an answer for that. I just want to do the cool things you can do."

She does not have the right mindset to be a soldier in the New Haven army.

A group of codexes approach us and mention there was an accident at a construction site where a group of people were fighting. Me, Hannah, and the codexes run over to the construction area. We get to the site where a suspension bridge is being built. This bridge will be a shortcut over a section of the woodlands to the nearest part of the railroad. Two construction workers are in each other's faces, and a group of men and women are standing around while a big strong man tries to defuse the situation.

"Guys, what's going on?" I ask the laborers.

One says, "He was disrespectful to me because I wasn't following his pace of work."

The other one shouts, "He is moving slow on purpose...to annoy me. Why doesn't he just work at the same pace we all work at?"

"What's more important, everyone? Making sure the bridge is built in record time? Or making sure it's safe to use for as long a time as possible?"

All the laborers look around and murmur amongst themselves. They all look exhausted.

"Everyone. All people who are working jobs to make New Haven a better place are tired. We are all doing good works. Everyone's role counts for something. The day is almost over. Let's all make peace and use that peace to finish today's work better. Tomorrow is another day to approach differently. But please no more fighting. Okay, guys?"

The laborer who is frustrated at the other worker grabs hold of his collar and starts screaming about how he is tired and wants to go home and see his kids. This is not needed at all. No excuse for him to grab the guy. No one else wants to step in because the laborer is so big. I step in and use my arms to create space between them. The angry laborer, in a fit of rage, grabs me, but I use his body weight against him to flip him to the ground. I put him in a submission hold and tell him to calm down. He finally calls uncle, and I release him.

Hannah is amazed at what she saw me do. The other workers express that he has temperament issues. I let some security detail know to keep an eye on him just in case he has another outburst.

I grab Hannah's hand and take her to the part of the Haven that is used for playing recreational activities. We go to an empty field and find a soccer ball that someone left behind for others to use. The recreational area of New Haven is a portion of town that is dedicated for people who need to take their minds off the seriousness of life. It's important to work hard but have fun sometimes, as well.

Me and Hannah kick the soccer ball to each other, trying to score in the opposite goal. While kicking the ball toward the goal, I trip, and Hannah takes the opportunity to score in my goal to win the game. I lie back down on the turf, and she falls next to me. We look at the cloudless sky.

"You think we will ever get back to the utopias of old, Lucy?"

"It's what I fight for. So I have to believe."

"What was Aelius like?"

"He was like the brother and best friend I never

had. Aelius was kind, honorable, and saw the good in things. He was a dreamer and visionary. I loved him so much. He was a codex who made me feel accepted more than any human being my age, at the time."

"I wish I could have gotten the chance to meet him."

"According to Aelius, there is a place where we will meet again, one day."

I walk Hannah back home and go to report for my next solo mission. This mission requirement is to go to the far south portion of our border and stand guard with other security cadets while our laborers work on a section that has been torn apart because of a heavy storm we received recently. The hurricane type conditions ripped a hole through the south end gate. This is an easy breach-point for the Zeros. TJ comes over to report for duty. I stand near the workers adding metal plates and thick pieces of wood to cover the gaping hole. I put the scope of my rifle to my eye and stay laser focused in the direction I need to be aware off. Danger happens fast and rarely holds back. So I need to be faster and one step ahead. While staying on scope, I see movement in the distance that seems like a threat. The crew is distracted because their lives are on the line at any moment, but I'm here, so it's okay. A Zero comes sprinting out from the brush, and I shoot her immediately in the legs. She screams in pain as I stand over her, pointing my assault rifle down at her. I need to put her out of her misery, but as I aim, I see myself as a little girl crying for someone to rescue me. I can't pull the trigger. TJ comes over and executes the Zero then looks at me weird. Some of the troops take the body away to burn it. I wipe sweat off my forehead, and I am frustrated that I could not finish the action I started.

I go back to being on scope. A few more try to breach, but we fire warning shots, and they run away. Which is what we are supposed to do if they charge without any weapons. This one had a baseball bat. Most of these Zeros lost their minds and are heavily radicalized against modern ways of being orderly and sophisticated. A few Zeros rush us again, but this time our warning shots did not phase them. They chase someone who was hammering nails, and the cadets have a hard time following behind.

"TJ, wait here. That's an order." I run after the Zeros and tackle one of them while the other cadets handle the other one. I drag the Zero by the leg back to the gate before he could reach the main areas of town, and the two cadets struggle with their captive beside me. Surprisingly, TJ listened to me and stood at watch. The Zero runs away, and I go over to grab the other Zero by the hair and yank him away from the two other struggling cadets. I take him to the ground outside the gap, and he runs away too.

The workers finish patching the south wall and are relieved their job is finished. I watch the laborers pack up their tools and thank me, TJ, and the other cadets. I walk away from everyone.

At home, I run a bath again, lower my body into the water, and submerge half my face. I hold my breath and close my eyes and see myself being abandoned, and how everyone wasn't fair to me during my military training. I go under water and hold my breath for as long as I can until my body trembles, and in that exact moment, I remember having to hold my breath for a prolonged amount of time in a river when a squad of codexes passes by, exterminating other people around me. I catch my breath and get out of the bathtub.

Tonight is the New Haven festival, marking the haven's anniversary of its existence. I sit on the roof of my home and make a paper airplane. I toss it in the direction of the festival. I climb down from my home and pick up my paper plane and walk into the festival. The only reason why Blackwater did not have me working all day and night into this festival is because, by law, he can only work me a certain number of shifts, which he already exhausted these last few days. If it weren't for that, I'd be somewhere with a loaded gun.

There are tables of foods that spread across the finest culture from different havens. Every Haven has a celebration like this during different points of the year. Representatives of the elders of other Havens take the trip here to give us gifts of resources, and we show hospitality. When it's time for their yearly celebration anniversary, we do the same.

The main streets are packed with people and codexes from all over Atlandia. Codexes have learned customary dances from the different human cultures of all the Havens. They dance with people from all around the nation. The music plays with passion and love. People are expressing their affection for each other by hugging and kissing. Codexes run about, playing with people in fun-filled activities. I find Lewis blowing bubbles for some children from different havens and making them laugh hysterically. I hug Lewis, and he hands me a bubble blower. The kids wait for me to blow more bubbles for them to chase and pop. They go running and yelling in different languages.

"Such a lively night," Lewis says.

"It is." Even during this lively celebration, I still scan my area for any threats.

Lewis knows this because I can't maintain eye contact with him. "Lucy, it's okay to let your guard down a little."

"I'll try, Lewis."

He takes my hand and smiles. "We both know you can try harder."

We walk around the festival, and I notice a few people coughing a lot and holding themselves as if expressing how they don't feel well. They call it a night. I watch them hobble off. I guess the cold is going around a little earlier than usual this year. A few codex units come over to me from other Havens and ask me to dance to a few songs with them. I tell them only if Lewis can join us.

"The medicine I took tonight is making me feel good. I can dance a little."

Me, Lewis, and the two codex units go to a cleared area where people are dancing around tall wooden fire-lit polls engraved with the freedom-abiding symbols of Atlandia. The codex units take my hands, and I follow as best I can to the rhythm and steps they make with their feet. They are doing better than me. I keep up with their dance moves, and Lewis starts keeping up too, but he grabs his lower back and walks off to the side to wait for me. The codexes and I hold hands and move around in a circle until I trip over my feet. The codex units pick me up. I see Lewis coughing like the other people from earlier. I leave the dance and run over to Lewis.

"I am fine, Lucy. I think I'm coming down with

a cold. Enjoy yourself tonight. Life is short."

"Okay, Lewis. Use that emergency radio I left for you to reach out to me, and I'll be there in an instant."

I sit down away from the dancing and watch everyone laughing, drinking, and enjoying each other's company. I am at a table near a bunch of men laughing and drinking. A codex from each Haven is with them, including one from mine. We had saved him on the recent extraction mission.

"Ah. Captain Lucy. Glad you can grace us with your presence. How are you enjoying the festivities?"

"I am trying to. A close friend tells me that I need to unwind. I've been through a lot."

The codex the platoon and I saved says, "Lucy is a very skilled soldier. I saw her do things that I haven't seen many others in the force do. She saved me from a camp of Zeros."

"From our Haven we heard stories about you, too. The missions you went on when collaborating with our troops. You must have had to outdo yourself through so much training beyond what was required."

I say to the guest codex, "More than anyone here would understand. There are a lot of people with skills and talents that I don't have. I won't sit here and say I am one of them. But no matter the mission I am tasked with, I will complete it or die."

Another foreign codex asks, "I believe that is

referred to as the human spirit and will, some of which we are grateful to possess. I enjoy very much how you expressed it."

"My human spirit and will is what kept me alive. As long as I draw breath, I will use it to fight for our freedom. The freedom of your kind and mine to live together in harmony. And the freedom of having the history we want to rewrite for ourselves."

A few people at nearby tables whistled and clapped after I said that. One comes over to offer me a beer. I raise my glass in the air, and so does everyone else.

"To the freedom to live," someone shouts.

We all shout in the name of Atlandia and drink. A few drinks later, I stumble out of the festival that will last until the next morning. I go into the wilderness safe zone where people from different havens are making out. There are no Zeros here. I continue to stumble around with the empty beer bottle in my hand, and it starts to rain lightly. I drop the bottle and lift my head up, letting the sprinkles of water hit my face. I stand here until the rain ends, and then I go back home.

The next morning, I am tasked with a mission. My head hurts a little from drinking, but duty calls. I step out and I see more people getting sick with the cold. I report to base, and Teddy Blackwater wants me to do a run until late at night again, even though newer recruits are supposed to do that and not captains, but that's neither here nor there.

I meet with the cadets at the west gate, which faces the direction of areas that have not been salvaged yet. There are a few abandoned towns that we need to go back to for valuable parts that would be hard for us to make ourselves. These cadets just came out of basic training and are ready to contribute to our society. The gates open, and we maneuver through the forest. At least these new recruits listen to me. The whole point of these runs is to get in and out fast so we don't have to encounter any Zeros.

We reach an abandoned town with a clock tower that still stands. I order one of the cadets to climb up there to scout for any threats.

She salutes and runs up the tower stairs.

Then I tell the other two cadets to watch each other's backs while patrolling the perimeter of the town. I wisely keep the last and youngest cadet with me. He is only seventeen years old. As we are combing through the rundown stores, he asks me a million questions about the stories he had heard about me and my records during training. I tell him to stay focused, that when danger happens, it comes when we least expect it. So we must be faster.

He hears what I am saying, but until he has to

commit to violence, he will never know. He tells me he will go and check a room in the small warehouse we are in. I watch him kick open the door and point his weapon in all corners of the room. We gather supplies, and I tell the cadet to hold the book bags while I take point. We leave the small warehouse, and I signal the clock tower to see if we are clear. She signals all clear.

Something doesn't feel right. It's too quiet. I don't know this area of the forest at all. The hairs on my neck stand up. I've only felt this way when facing death.

I signal the cadet on the clock tower to come down. I tell the cadets patrolling the area to come back to us.

"Are you sure you didn't see anything up there?"

"No, captain."

"Everyone, let's take cover behind these stacks of tires. Quickly. Let's go."

We get behind cover and see Zeros with codex units holding blunt objects walk into the town.

Why are codexes with them?

And they are holding weapons. They hit random objects with their bats and pipes, making noises. The codexes are just copying the Zeros and think this is the way they are supposed to act.

The Zeros must have caught these codex units

during their march back into human civilization and kept them from seeing progress in the world. This is not good. I have flashbacks to when I had to evade codexes the minute I saw just one, and here there are three with three Zeros. I look over at the cadets' faces, and they are concerned and waiting on my orders to get us out of this situation.

"Captain, what do we do?"

"Stay here and only come out when I say."

"But, captain..."

I stand up and point my rifle at them. The Zeros come running to me with their weapons in hand, and within seconds, I put them all down. The three codex units don't move.

"Why were you with these Zeros?" I shout. "Where are you from? Answer now."

A codex says, "We are Zeros. We were told that the old ways are what is best for our kind. Your kind is very complicated, so these humans made everything simple. After the bright blue flash, we found your kind here and adjusted to their ways."

"Their ways are wrong. Man and codex live in peace once more. I can show you."

The codexes look at the Zeros lying in pools of blood. "These were our friends. You terminated them?" They make fists.

This isn't good. How did the Zeros hack into

codex mainframes? Were they trying to manipulate the codex we'd retrieved on that rescue mission?

"Stand down. This isn't your kind's legacy anymore. If you come closer, I will terminate all of you."

The codex units walk toward me, and I fire warning shots into the ground at their feet.

"I said stop, or the next shots will terminate you."

For a moment, the codex units look like they will surrender. They slowly put their hands in the air. My cadets break cover.

"I told all of you to stay behind cover," I shout to them.

The codex units charge us, and by the time I turn back to them, I barely dodge one of their weapons. I get grazed in the face and hear ringing in my ears. The cadets shoot and miss most of their shots but run to them and take their weapons. One of the cadets falls into a fetal position and cries.

I lower my gun and terminate the codex unit that hit me. With the safety of my team in mind, I terminate the remaining codexes. They all drop, and their lights turn off.

The cadets all have shocked looks on their faces.

One of the codexes did not go offline right away and is crawling on the ground toward a blunt object a Zero was going to use against us. I step on the codex and execute him.

I slap the cadet who is crying in a fetal position and yank him to his feet and shake him. “Snap out of it. Help the others grab the resources we found and let’s move out.”

The cadets are quiet as they quickly organize everything and get their bearings. As we walk back to New Haven, I feel bad for how harsh I was with them. “Hey, guys. I am sorry for lashing out after that skirmish. This is all new for you guys.”

“I understand, Captain Lucy. We still have a lot of experience to gain before we are as comfortable as you are in those situations.”

The female cadet says, “I joined the force because of the legendary missions I heard you went on and what you’re able to do.”

“Let’s get back from our run safely, and then we will talk more.” This time they listen to everything I say, as we are in Haven territory. My face hurts from that smack the codex gave me, and now I have a bruised eye that hurts.

The guards let us in and they look at me in shock. They have never seen me with a black eye before. At base, TJ looks at me and smirks, knowing I have this mark on my face. We report to Blackwater who is spinning his revolver, reading documents that look like they are in another language. When he sees us he puts the documents down and flips them over hastily like he didn't want us to see them.

"Sir, we have completed our run and brought back resources for the good of New Haven."

"How did you get the mark on your face?"

"I was struck by a codex unit who was accompanying a group of Zeros that attacked us. I have never seen codexes part of the Zeros. We should let the rest of the departments know right away."

Blackwater looks at me with a disgusted sneer. He yells at the cadets to get back to their tasks and tells me to stay in place. "Is this some sort of joke? A codex unit acting violently toward us? And with those wild animals?"

"It's not a joke."

"I am ashamed to say this, but I think your career as a soldier may come to an end soon. You're having irrational thoughts and imagining things that are impossible while on a simple run. If you ever mention something like that again, and if I hear that you've told anyone else your joke, I'll demote you. You're dismissed. Now get out of my sight."

I clench my jaw and salute and march away angry and wanting to scream. I hold it in until I get home and shout at the top of my lungs. I grab a pack of ice and place it over my eye. I keep the ice pack compressed on my eye and sit down to stare out the window at people walking around, going about their day. By now, at least a thousand people populate each Haven. I do what I do for the freedom of these people and codexes alike. I will always keep fighting the good fight. Even with this black eye.

I hear some commotion and stress outside my home. I step out and see someone on the ground, unconscious. A group of people gather. I look at one of our own struggling to breathe. I shout for someone to get the local doctor while I radio for emergency assistance.

Medical personnel arrive at the scene and stabilize the person. I ask the medic what's going on with people's health. He tells me there's an infection going around and that my friend Lewis is in the hospital, fighting for his life. They take the person away.

I go to the hospital to check on Lewis. I am sure he can use some company. I walk into the hospital, and Debra comes running over to me in the lobby, crying.

"Lewis is not doing well, and the nurses kicked me out of his room because of the danger of spreading the infection. He is in so much pain, and it's killing me that I can't be there for him."

"I will find out what's going on with Lewis."

His room is in a quarantined status, which means

nobody is allowed in the room except for doctors and authorized military personnel. Not even I can walk in there without providing documentation.

As the day goes along, the guards on patrol dwindle to only one doing perimeter patrol. I have the advantage of night to sneak into Lewis's room. I go back to the hospital, wearing all black and climb up the outside wall while the guard isn't around. I pick the window lock to Lewis's room as quietly as I can and step in.

Lewis is hooked into many machines monitoring his body. Everything in this room is covered in plastic. I barely recognize Lewis. His skin is covered with black rotting blots.

I need to hold back from crying so the nurses working the night shift won't know I am here. If I get caught, I will get demoted, for sure. I take pride in being a captain for our home forces. I carefully place a chair down beside Lewis.

He opens his eyes halfway. They are bloodshot red. "What a nice surprise." I reach for his hand but he moves it away. "No. Don't touch me or you might get infected with this disease. How did you get the shiner?"

"It is nothing, don't worry. There must be something they can do to make this infection go away."

"No. I am ready to accept my fate and leave this world. I escaped death before because of what most consider divine intervention from Aelius. I should have died years ago, Lucy."

He coughs up blood, and I give him a napkin.

"If my children were alive today you would have been the best aunt to them. I know I was hard on you when you were younger and you preferred to be around Michael and Debra. I am sorry for that. I was in a bitter place. You spent so much of your life being a protector and serving the people of New Haven without focusing on doing other things that make you happy. War will never go away for as long as people exist. Lucy, you still have a lot of life ahead of you. Start thinking about the next chapters and maybe even starting a family."

I wipe my tears. This will probably be the last time I talk to him. "Okay, Lewis. I will."

Lewis smiles and winks. He passes out, and the monitors hooked into him flatline. I watch Lewis take his final long breath before passing away. "Goodbye, Lewis. I will miss you."

I hear footsteps approaching the room. I put the chair back exactly where it was, open the window, and climb down to the ground where I hide in the bushes as the guard comes back around on his patrol.

I leave the hospital and sit at the local pub and

stare at my beverage with white foam sitting on top of golden-brown malt. I wipe my eyes, swallow some painkillers, and wash them down with the beer. Around me are people escaping from their pains. The codex bartender asks me if I want another drink. We use codexes to do this work because they can see people's vitals, and know if they've had one too many.

"Yes, please."

I take another handful of painkillers and wash it down, and my body starts to feel warm and numb.

"I am sorry. But I can only offer you one more malt beverage."

"That's fine. Thank you."

The bartender hands me the beverage and smiles at me as my eyes well up. I go to take the last of my painkillers, but the codex stops me.

"Too much of that can stop your heart."

"My heart is already broken."

"If your heart is broken you should go to the hospital. Do you want me to take you? I'm closing the bar in a few."

"I don't need the hospital. But I can use some company at the lake."

The codex bartender and I sit on a bench at the shore of the lake that is in the center of New Haven.

"I used to come here with a friend to stare at the stars reflecting off the water. He passed away tonight.

And my heart is broken. Do you know what I mean?"

"I am sorry for your loss. Death can be very heavy, and having company helps a lot. I am here to keep you company. What was his name?"

I wipe my eyes. "Lewis. He was like an uncle to me. He found me when I was left for dead in the wilderness during the times of the old ways."

"I am sorry for what my kind did."

"Don't apologize. You didn't do anything. Your company right now means a lot."

"We are the family of New Haven. Through life and death. We support each other."

The next day at Lewis's funeral, I sit next to Debra, consoling her, the same way the codex helped me process my feelings last night. Lewis's body had to be burned right after he died because of the risk of infection. Instead of an open casket, a tribute is made for him. It is New Haven custom to have a choir in the front. They sing traditional New Haven songs of peace and safe travels to life hereafter. We are all a family here that adds to the human and codex story.

Debra says, "Lewis was misunderstood by most people because of how guarded he was. But once you got past that guard, he was there for you no matter what."

"I remember when Michael and Lewis rescued me when the group I used to travel the wilderness with abandoned me. At that time I couldn't believe they were real."

My hands are shaking as I remember that traumatic moment of being left for dead in a world where codexes hunted people.

Debra puts her hands on mine, and they stop shaking. I watch people of our community lay flowers and other artistic crafts around his casket. Lewis served in the original armed forces while Joseph was Elder. I hope he is in a place of peace and reunited with his children. I remember how distraught and bitter he used to be. I am so happy he found peace before he died. Although, something isn't right with how he died. Yeah. He had physical issues, but this disease came out of nowhere. I've never seen anything like it before.

After the funeral, I go to the target range to take my mind off everything. I hit every target without fail. I take a crossbow and line up my shot. As I aim, scenes from the nightmare I had recently played in my mind. The roaring sands in the fallen city and that mysterious codex unit grabbing my neck causes me to shoot the arrow and miss my target completely. I put the crossbow down and rub the sides of my head. I keep having that dream in the ruins of Paradise and being chased by an ominous codex figure. I leave the range and go for a jog around the perimeter of New

Haven. As I jog, I gaze up at the sky where I want to be for my next travels. I see myself back in my plane, leaving a streak in the sky.

After running a few miles, I get down and do push ups. I need to keep my body in the best shape possible to carry out my duties, regardless of how difficult Blackwater can be. Each time my body lowers to the floor and raises I think about how he mistreats me. While doing pushups, I hear someone ask me if there is any more space at the hospital. I gasp when seeing the rotting black marks on this person's flesh and bloodshot eyes. He coughs up some blood, and I immediately signal for transportation personnel to take him to medical care. New Haven has a public transit system that we are trying to make like the old metropolis's mass transit.

I walk around the city and see people are coughing and in pain all around me. Is this from the same virus Lewis had? Just a few hours ago everyone was fine. But now the streets of New Haven are a mess with illness. This illness is sucking away the bustling spirit that my home radiates.

At the hospital, General Blackwater and other high-ranked officers go inside. Dozens of tents are set up as extra space for medical attention. Something drastic is going on. Elder Michael comes over to me.

"Lucy, we need to talk."

Chapter 2

It has been a few weeks since the viral outbreak plagued my home, and now that winter has arrived, the infection rate is increasing. Many people died from this unknown plague that our doctors and scientists can't figure out. The longer it takes them to classify the disease, the longer it will take to create a vaccine for the good people of New Haven.

This winter is the harshest we have recorded. Record temps at the freezing mark with heavy snow that has not stopped accumulating, which requires a lot of shoveling. There is a quarantine in effect so people must remain a certain distance away from each other and must follow the curfew set in place.

Elder Michael did not want to resort to this, but right now it is the only method to slow down infection. My home is not the same. The Zeros have been taking the opportunity to attack our walls, knowing we are weakened. Our fighters are tired of the constant shifts and fights against the Zeros that use codexes now, and people are wondering why, and everyone is scared.

The other Havens haven't been as gracious to us with their railroad trade of valuables and goods. They see us as a failing state that can potentially bring them all down. Which is sad because we are supposed to be united, but now that we are faced with a new challenge, they abandon us. I don't like that, and something needs to be done about it. New Haven was the first to help others when they needed it the most. We do this because we stand for freedom and the future.

The other soldiers I am on border patrol duty with keep talking about what our General and Elder are doing to fix the strife we are in. They don't sound too hopeful. Morale isn't high. The soldiers also complain about how they are required to pull back-to-back doubles because some of the other guards who were supposed relieve us got sick.

"Come on, guys. Remember why we do this. If we give up then everyone else will, too."

The two younger guards stop complaining.

I give them a few love-taps on the helmet and encourage them. One of them mentions how his younger brother, Carl, is badly sick and is alone. I tell cadet 757 I will go and spend time with him. I search the medical tents spread out all over the place with nurses and other volunteers running around for extra supplies. It is so chaotic here. I find the medical tent where his little brother is, and he is in critical condition. He has the black blotches all over him, and he is barely breathing.

"Hey, can you hear my voice? I am your friend. Lucy. I know your older brother."

He slowly moves his head to look at me. "You are friends with my big brother? I love him so much. He is the bravest big brother ever."

"Is there anything you need right now?"

"I never got to add the last car model to my collection. I almost completed it. But there is a bright red car I didn't get the chance to add to my shelf. It's like one of the red sports cars that our ancestors use to race."

"I'll get you that car if you promise me to keep being strong and fighting."

I get back to the group I am on watch with and tell cadet 757 I need to take care of something quickly.

"How's Carl holding up?"

"He is strong and fighting."

I leave New Haven and travel to a small town that used to be a busy shopping area. This mall is generally off limits because it is used as a main hub for Zeros. I check my ammunition and feel confident with me being here alone even if there are codexes now joining the Zeros' forces. I must assume there are only a handful of codexes compared to people who are Zeros because most codexes joined the Haven states at the beginning of Atlandia's conception.

I enter a three-level mall and point my rifle scope in all directions. I take a broken pipe and toss it in front of me and get behind a broken picture-taking machine. The pipe skips across the floor and echoes throughout the mall. No Zeros come running out.

After waiting for a couple minutes, I continue inside as quietly as I can. The escalator doesn't work anymore, and I don't plant my foot too hard on the steps, so I don't make unnecessary noise. I go into the abandoned toy store and find everything here is destroyed. I rummage through the rubble and hear footsteps from the entrance of the mall. A group is sprinting up the escalator.

I quickly duck behind a shelf of broken toys and peek around with my hand on my gun, ready to shoot. A group of Zeros disperse around the mall. I see they're with one codex unit. I wait for the coast to clear and go to the Top Cars store I remember hearing about from other runners who passed by here before. I find the red car for Carl and put it in my backpack that has more bullets and blades. I hear conversation down the hall in the mall.

I leave the toy car shop and crouch down to get closer to the conversations. A few more Zeros enter a rundown clothing store. I maneuver behind some clothes and see the Zeros are all in a circle, talking about how they need to keep doing good for their leader. I didn't think they had a leader. One Zero mentions how this codex unit promised them dominance over the world as long as they continue to be patient and keep doing what they are doing. Another Zero mentions how this god-like codex is meant to come back for them. That their way of life is the true way and not what Atlandia is doing.

Who are they talking about?

I make my retreat but my foot steps on a plastic shirt hanger and cracks it.

They all turn around and look in all directions.

Now I know I can't sneak my way out. I have to be loud and make a run for it. I take three deep breaths, reveal myself, shoot, and run back from where I came. Every few seconds, I turn back to shoot a short burst of rounds to make my pursuers duck for cover. I run a zig zag course as objects are thrown my way. A few moments later, I'm running a safe distance away from the mall.

I sit on the side of a dirt road and hold the red racing car toy in my hands. I know Carl will love this. He just needs to keep being strong for me. I walk back in the direction of New Haven and hear someone running. I turn around and see it's that codex from the mall, running hard and fast.

I aim on scope, and when I shoot, my gun jams. I keep trying shoot but all I hear are clicks, and the codex is only a few feet away from me. I throw my rifle to the side and draw my combat blade.

The codex goes down on her knees with hands raised.

I lower my guard and go to her, but the moment I get there, she strikes me in the gut so hard I lose my breath. While I am trying to regain my wind, she swings at me wildly, and I do my best to evade but take the blows here and there. Even though I'm using my arms to protect myself, the codex's strikes feel like a metal bat hitting me.

I run away to buy me just enough time to take out my grenade. As soon as I turn the codex grabs me by the neck and lifts me off my feet. Using my combat knife I stab into the part of the codex that isn't thick metal and create an opening. With my other hand, I take the pin out of the grenade and shove it into the hole I made. Using my both my feet, I push myself out of the codex's grip and dive forward just as the grenade explodes. I take some of the blast as parts of the codex hit me. If I hadn't dived out of the way, I would have been blown up too. I catch my breath and notice a portion of the toy car is crushed from the fight. I walk over to the pieces of codex and kick them around in anger. I am sure Carl will appreciate the car, regardless of its condition. I hurry back to his medical tent and I see a body bag being taken out of his area. I ask a medic, "Where is Carl? I spoke to him only a couple hours ago."

"He passed away."

I put my head down and walk back to watch the cadets. Cadet 757 is being consoled by those around him. I hand him the damaged red toy car and he holds it with both hands and cries over it. I don't say anything and walk to the hospital and check in with the front desk clerk. I tell her I just want to walk around. She allows it for only a few minutes, since Blackwater has the area quarantined for his top-priority fighters.

Lewis's patient room now houses a couple who I would see around town, always holding hands. Now they're lying on separate hospital beds, breathing heavily. Nurses are tending to them, but it seems like they won't make it either.

Medics scurry around to respond to emergencies as I can do nothing but wonder why this is happening to our home. I see an elderly woman being helped by someone, and I follow them. They take her to the lake to see it for the last time, as she is aware of her last hours. I shake my head and walk away.

I go to Lewis's home that had to be closed off

from a family being able to move in. At the side of the house are some flowers that have withered away. A codex comes beside me and places a worn pair of shoes at his tribute.

I look at him curiously. "How did you know Lewis?"

"Lewis spared my life years ago. According to what I heard. I am the first codex he did not terminate during the great Unison. That is an honor. These shoes were his old ones he used for his runs outside the walls."

"I miss him."

"I can understand why you do. When we create impactful memories with someone, they leave a long-lasting impression. That impression will stay with us forever."

"That was beautiful."

"I had a codex friend who was terminated during the transition from the old to the new ways. I think about my friend everyday. I loved my friend so much and will live the rest of my life online remembering my friend. Love doesn't have a shelf life. Not like we are made in the image of God."

I get a call on the radio to report to a portion of the train line outside of New Haven to provide security for the engineers. The harshness of winter messes with tracks and requires repairs. At the mission site with TJ and the usual group of cadets, I keep my eyes peeled for any anomalies happening around us. The Zeros have become very efficient at attacking through the tree lines. When dealing with them, one cannot hesitate because they don't.

TJ takes my position in our tactical formation, and I stand beside the engineers breaking the ice that developed on the train track so they can do the electrical repairs. I hear footsteps in the snow coming our way. The cadets and I quickly turn our attention to the footsteps, ready to execute a lethal maneuver.

Hannah runs out from the tree line. "Lucy, I finally get to be on a cool mission with you." She wields a small blade and looks around for any potential threats as if she is on the mission with us.

"Hannah. You know you are not supposed to be here."

"It's not fair. Mom and Dad want me to be cooped up inside, but I want to explore. I want to have fun."

I tell my platoon to remain at this position while I escort Hannah back to safety. I take her hand and walk into the snowy wilderness. She has no idea how much danger she has put herself in.

"Are you going to tell my mom and dad that I came to see you? Please don't."

"Just stay close to me and keep your voice down.

We are going back now."

I hear movements in the snow, so I stop and get us low behind a tree. This tree has a deep split in it, so I tell Hannah to squeeze her way in there temporarily. I level my rifle as two Zeros charge at me. I shoot both in the legs, and they drop into the deep snow. The white snow now has red streaks on it. A few more come at me from multiple angles but I shoot them non-lethally. A Zero manages to get a hold of me from behind and throws my rifle off into the snow. I use my close quarter combat skills to defend myself by landing vicious strikes.

I remain in a kickboxing stance as three more Zeros come out from the white void of snow-covered trees. Everything slows down, including the snow flakes floating downward. I reach at the side of my boot and pull out my combat knife. One-by-one, I spill their blood all over the once pure white snow.

After I take care of the enemy, I retrieve my rifle.

Hannah is terrified by what she witnessed me do. This is the reality of our world. We must kill to protect the ones we love. I reach out to soothe Hannah but pull my hands back when I see blood on them. "Let's go. We can't stay here."

At the front gates of New Haven Debra runs over to us and embraces her daughter.

"Your father will not be happy about this. How

much trouble did you cause?" Debra sees the blood all over my hands. "I am sorry, Lucy. This won't ever happen again."

A few guards escort her into the city.

Debra hands me a towel to wipe the blood off. "Lucy, I am so sorry she caused you to resort to violence. I won't ask what you had to do. She will not be leaving the city for a while. She is punished."

"Go easy on her. I was just like her. Curious about the world. Except she has a mother and father to watch over her. She will be alright."

I wipe the wet blood off as best I can and go back to the mission site. Just up ahead, my guys are at their posts with the track workers. Before I go to them, I hide behind a tree and cry as quietly as I can. Although I am trained to protect New Haven people, property, and policy, that doesn't mean it doesn't affect me after a while.

I compose myself and go into formation with the cadets until we complete our mission and escort the track workers back to safety. The engineers express gratitude for safe passage back home.

I go back to base, and in the washroom, I wash the dried blood off my hands with soap and water. Even though my hands are clean, the battle stains will always remain. I have had to kill many people and codexes during my time as a soldier. The act of killing has gotten easier, but over time it has had an effect on me. My skillset allows me to be comfortable in life-threatening situations. But when I am the one taking life, human or codex, I feel like a small part of me dies with them.

General Blackwater calls me to his office, and I stand at attention before him. Instead of letting me know that I did a great job with the hiccup in our escort mission, he tells me about the summit meeting tomorrow and to be sure I am on point with everything. I notice a folder under his armpit with a classified stamp on it and the name Aelius. He notices that I see it and locks it away in a file cabinet. After he finishes briefing me, I leave, but from behind a rack of weapons, I hold back to watch all the officers exit his office. Teddy walks out and stations a woman deputy at his door. Blackwater leaves the building while the deputy stands guard. I follow Blackwater to make sure he leaves the base. I hurry back to his office and approach the rookie guard.

"Captain Lucy, it's good to see you."

"Thank you, deputy. I could have sworn I heard a group of cleaners saying they need your assistance accessing the supply closet down in B level. How about you go see what they need? In the meantime, I'll stand watch for you here."

"Roger that, captain, I'll be right back."

She leaves the area, and I immediately pick the lock to Blackwater's office. Inside, I don't move or touch anything that may cause the general to be suspicious. I pick the lock to his file cabinet. I carefully flip folders and find the classified one. I place the file on his desk and open it. Inside are very detailed drawings of the Paradise ruins. Some photographs are included, and in the pictures, a mysterious figure is present. Is that a person or a codex? Nobody is allowed at the ruins, so I wonder if Blackwater took these photos without anyone knowing.

Beside these photos are his writings. I recognize his handwriting anywhere. I read letters about finding a codex unit who will grant him access to unbelievable power from the remains of an overseer. These letters express the want to abandon his authority of a haven general and usher in a foreign and extreme system onto the world. The letters become more deranged and obsessive. The hand writing gets harder to read. Something is seriously wrong with this.

Is Blackwater going to betray us?

All these letters have the same dates where he was supposedly busy doing private obligations. He kept visiting the Paradise ruins to meet with someone. Probably exchanging information in secrecy.

I put everything back the way I found it and lock

the cabinet. I exit his office and lock the door. The deputy comes back and resumes her post.

The next day, Elder Michael elects me to be his right wing during the quarterly national summit. The national summit is where all twelve Elders of the nation congregate at town hall to discuss politics and the state of the nation. Michael and I board the train. These locomotives are a lifeline that gives us a chance to be a full-fledgling nation. Without the railroads, it would take days by foot to reach the other haven states.

Michael says, "I heard the trouble my daughter caused you. That won't happen again."

"I just didn't want her getting hurt."

"She reminds me of how you were. Always wanting to leave the safety zone. But I never was that worried about you because of how quickly you grew into handling yourself."

"The other captains are not happy you picked me so soon when you did. Even if I can handle myself just fine."

"I picked you because you are the most skilled. They won't admit that. The truth is you are probably our most talented soldier."

I look out the window, watching the snowy trees pass by us at top speeds. As the trees whip by, I think about what I found in the general's office. I close my eyes and take a breath. And there are the weird dreams I have at the codex ruins. Michael can clearly see that my thoughts are all over the place.

"Lucy. Let's go to the back of the train where there is more privacy. Plus I can use some fresh air."

Michael tells the guards that we will be going to the last car where there is an outdoor platform. We stand on the small platform, and Michael leans on the handrails. "So you had the same dream Debra and I had about the forgotten ruins of Paradise. What do you make of that? I think fate has something big in store for us once again."

"I don't know what to make of it. All I know, there is a foreign threat we can't identify yet."

"The harshness of winter and the plague that struck us seems like it is coming from something that is supernatural."

Michael learned to be very spiritual and philosophical like Joseph used to be. I don't get too deep into philosophy like Michael does. He believes in purpose from a higher power and spiritual mysteries beyond our comprehension. Like fate or destiny. Why would spiritual mysteries cause this chaos within our home?

The train docks at the terminal. I stay close to Michael the entire walk throughout the capital. Town hall is located in the center of Atlandia and is made of marble and other precious metals with sculptures of important people and objects from the past that we strive to recreate into a new future. Influential leaders in history along with society-advancing inventions are made of white marble and are set on each side of the long white marble steps to the congressional house that looks like a castle. During the medieval times of our history, people lived in giant castles. It's not quite the same castles like medieval times, but it resembles the architecture. Inside the capitol are high ceilings with giant paintings of memorable events in our history, portraits of heroes who have shaped our lives, and artwork of the utopias from way back.

We all enter a dimly lit room with a long table. The judges, who mediate and document all political talks, light the candles on the table and greet us. All the Elders sit in their respective places at the table with their right wings by their right shoulder. The junior judges stand near us with paper and pen ready to document what will be discussed for record purposes and legislation.

Judges and junior judges are appointed as the official recorders and mediators of law and decree for the nation. They are of the same social status and possess similar legal powers as an Elder. General Blackwater enters the room and stands by the front doors with the other Havens' military leaders.

Blackwater looks at me like he would rather see me drop dead, and I look at him the same way. The lead mediating judge sits at the head of the table and taps it twelve times.

"Today we gather to discuss policies and affairs with one another for the betterment of the country. Before we begin, I will do the customary greeting of all the Fathers and Mothers of Havens. Elder Michael of New Haven. Elder Matthew from Emerald Haven. Elder John from Marine Haven. Elder Thomas from Mountain Haven. Elder Eduardo from Sand Haven. Elder Bak from Gold Haven. Elder Dominik from Grassland Haven. Elder Singh-Lee from North Haven. Elder Agatha from Mist Haven. Elder Gresha from South Garden Haven. Elder Darnell from Sapphire Haven. Welcome all."

The panel goes down the list discussing essential topics from least importance to high priority. After long negotiations and agreements with the laws, all Elders besides Michael stand up regarding an issue. The mediator gets a note handed to him.

"It seems we have an issue on hand that won't allow our meeting to end on fair terms. An infection spreads rapidly through New Haven and the other Elders are worried about their safety."

Michael places his hands flat on the table then reveals his palms as a customary sign of exposing any truths that need to be brought up immediately.

"Based on what I am reading. Michael. You must acknowledge the severity of this situation right now to us all."

"It is true. My Haven has been struck by a plague that we haven't gotten full control over."

The judge says, "On behalf of the panel in this sacred meeting, we all want to know what measures must take place from your end to ensure the illness doesn't become a pandemic."

Michael smiles and stands, showing his palms. "My fellow Elders of this country. I do have an idea that will cure the plague."

I look at Michael confused. He never mentioned anything about a cure to me.

The lead judge asks, "And how do you go about creating this cure?"

"Destiny."

Murmurs go around the room.

"I know all of you have your doubts, but after the gift we received decades ago, I've come to believe in miracles beyond our physical understanding. Let us not forget the events when Aelius was with us and the things that went beyond what technology could explain. Give me some more time to continue my research, and I promise this will all go away."

One Elder says, "Michael, with all respect. We

don't feel any more comfortable with your response."

Another Elder says, "I wouldn't want to hold off on our usual business trades because of your faith in the spiritual mysteries. I can't risk my people being in harm's way. Science and technology are the only way to ensure safety."

Elder Matthew from Emerald Haven sits back down, having shown verbally that he is not on the same page as the other Elders, nor in agreement with the measures they are willing to implement. Michael and Matthew have always been the closest of friends compared to the other Elders.

The other leaders talk amongst each other, throwing out threats of closing off their borders, trade routes with us, and having to vote on a hard quarantine with our people.

Michael believes so much in the spiritual mysteries that his answers aren't concrete enough to give everyone, including me, confidence in a hopeful and swift outcome.

The lead judge tells us, "Based on what I am hearing and for the betterment of the United Havens of Atlandia, a deadline will be put into effect. Elder Michael, you have a month to show all of us that proactive measures are taking place to handle this situation and not just philosophical wonderings. Next courses of actions and consequences will be voted on by all members of the board to decide the fate of New Haven's continuing existence or deconstruction. Pleasure speaking to all of you. This panel is dismissed."

I follow behind Michael, Matthew, and his right wing in the grand halls of parliament. General Blackwater and some troops walk by, and I look at him with suspicious eyes, and he catches on. He keeps walking. I shake Elder Matthew's hand and tap right elbows with his right wing as a sign of respect.

Matthew says to Michael, "Things got intense in there, my friend. Tell me what's going on."

"My home is crumbling. The Zeros have been taking advantage of our vulnerable state because our forces are sick. Things are worse than what I led on. I just had to let the other Elders know it is not that bad because of the threats. So much has happened in our species history, and at the same time, nothing has changed at all."

"Do you really have an idea for a cure? Or was that just to cover yourself? Please be honest with me because I will do what I can to help my brother."

Michael looks around at the giant portraits and paintings of key moments that have happened in human history. "History repeats itself. And we must do what we can to push the needle a little farther while treasuring the ones we love."

"Michael, please. Give me something to hold onto so I can help because my voice does not surpass an official voting."

"Allow Lucy to enter your Haven. She's not sick. Part of my answer for a cure is in your underground emerald caverns at the ancient archaeological mines. My response to why I believe is because of the mysteries of our world. That's the best I can give you, brother."

"Of course, Michael. I just hope that helps."

Michael and I walk down the white marble steps.

"Lucy. The dreams I, you, and Debra had are not a coincidence. Fate is knocking on our door again just like when Aelius came into our life. You saw the glowing tree, right?"

"Yes."

"All of our dreams ended in the presence of the divine tree. I believe that tree holds the cure to eliminating the plague that can potentially cripple our continent. During my research and what I documented from my dream, the ancient emerald caverns are said to have a tablet that holds coordinates to a tree that grows fruit that has properties that can cure any illness. A tree of life so to speak. Our modern medicine has no answer. We need to rely on our faith.

"I could not tell the other elders this because they will think that old Michael has lost his mind. I believe something related to the events of Aelius are happening again. After you come back from Emerald Haven, we need to go to the desert ruins of Paradise even if it is off limits. When the time is right we will take your plane and fly over there. Head over to Emerald Haven first and get back to me with what you find."

I watch Michael get escorted by our forces, and I step into a train heading to Emerald Haven. General Blackwater glowers at me, disgusted that I'm going to another Haven. I close the window blinds on him inside the train car and take a deep breath. Maybe Michael is right. Something out of our control is happening again. Throughout our human history many illnesses have come and gone. Some far worse than others. Back in the dark ages where people rode horses, pre-electricity era, the bubonic plague came and wiped out more than half of the population. But life found a way to hold on. The will power of Atlandia will survive this too.

At the gates of Emerald Haven, I marvel at the green precious metals everywhere. Engraved in the emerald gates are the codes the people here live by. The gates open, and I step into Emerald Haven where they have green cobblestone roads and pathways going all over the place. Groups of people are singing in pockets of the city. The songs are traditional

Atlandia songs of grace and power. The choir's voices are so beautiful like the architecture of this city. It's no wonder why people here have their spirits in a positive way. Then again they aren't going through what we are. The music and art here is exploding in genius. The city is known for its culture and value in the artistic mediums more than any other haven. They believe that our species will make its next steps through creativity and beauty. From what I read in the schools' history books, art and culture play a vital role in a civilization's longevity as a sustained diverse society. Atlandia is multicultural in the same way. As the right wing escorts me throughout the towns, people look at me with caution, thinking that I am infected with the plague. This is an odd feeling of other people to see me as a disease to the planet. Every citizen moves out of the way and covers their mouths.

"I wonder if this is how all Havens look at us."

"Try to ignore them. They are scared about the threats that can harm our better ways of living. I am sure you can't blame them. New Haveners would do the same if someone who they heard was infected came by."

"True. But we would not stand by and watch another Haven fall apart. But New Haven is resilient. We will find a way."

"I have a lot of respect for you, captain. But we all need some help."

At the ivory palace, Matthew gets up from his throne and signals his guards to take a resting position. The right wing who escorted me here does their salute and takes a step back away from me.

"Lucy, I hear that you're an outstanding soldier. New Haven is blessed to have you on their force. I promised Michael I would do anything I can to help your situation back east. How may I be of service?"

"Thank you for your kind words, Elder Matthew. Elder Michael has requested that I be allowed privileges to explore your ancient ruins. Michael says part of his solution will be found there."

Matthew signals his guards to come by my side. "I will grant your request. Although I am not sure what is in those caves that will contribute to such a complex problem that New Haven is dealing with."

"I trust my Elder on his decision to send me here."

His team escorts me to their archeological site of caves and catacombs where scientists and miners work together to dig through rocks to find artifacts of the ancient world. Michael believes that the answers for our future can be found in the distant past. Michael also told me that there is a specific wall with a forgotten language inscribed on it, and to keep an eye out for it. These caves seem like they can go all the way to the center of the planet.

I sweat from a surge of emotions and something tugging on my body. I stop walking with the guards and feel a magnetic force pulling me to a portion of the mines that no archaeologists are studying.

"Lucy of New Haven. Is everything okay?"

"Yes. I think so. I need to go down that way."

"Most of the uncovered artifacts are in the opposite area of the mines."

"I understand. But please escort me this way."

The vibrations intensify within me while standing in front of this flat sheet of emerald that has chunks of rock on it. The guards are very confused as to why we are here. They explain that the miners have no use for this slab of emerald and granite because some of the symbols they tried to decipher don't add up to anything.

I raise my hand to it and feel a slight tug on my fingertips. It's like my skin is being stretched to embrace it. I plant my palm on the emerald sheetrock, and the symbols rearrange to become a language I can interpret. This emerald tablet specifically instructs me, Michael, and Debra to return to the ruins of Paradise and stand in the middle of the rubble where the false god used to rule this world.

I remove my hand, and the emerald tablet moves

back to the way it was.

The guards are scratching their heads as if wondering what I am doing.

"We can leave now," I say.

The guards escort me out of the mines, and I tell them to give Elder Matthew the message that I got what I needed and to thank him.

Back home at New Haven, I sit on a bench overlooking the river that cuts through the middle of our city. The twilight golden light reflects off the water. Michael and Debra sit by my side on the bench.

"Such a beautiful sight," Michael says.

I say to them, "The tablet reads that we have to go back to Paradise."

Debra says, "And stand in the rubble where the false god used to rule."

"How did you know that, Debra?"

Michael tells me, "I did not tell you the rest of our dreams because I needed to be sure that the supernatural is occurring once more at our home. The fact that the emerald tablet gave you that message, and our dreams align with the message, tells me for certain that there are moving parts going on behind the scenes that we need to uncover. Our world may depend on it again."

I clutch the seashell necklace the kids made for me when I first got back. I don't like relying on these types of philosophical wonderings Michael likes to talk about. People are sick and not getting better, so we need medicine, not spiritual talk.

"Whatever is going on we can't let the world fall back to the old ways. Not after Aelius gave his gift to us."

Debra says, "We all agree, Lucy."

"General Blackwater won't authorize me to use the aircraft again to leave New Haven property. I'm still a soldier under his command."

"And I am the Elder and will overrule his orders. And if he and I must go before a judge, I will risk my title of Elder."

Before I tell Michael about my findings regarding Teddy, we hear an explosion. Everyone around us stops walking to look at the big cloud of black smoke in the direction of the military base. We have never seen an explosion that big within our walls.

At the base, there is a large gaping hole in one of the hangers and everything is on fire. Two more explosions happen in the direction of the southern gate. We are under attack and there is no sign of our General. I immediately go to help many injured soldiers. We see a fighter craft fly over us. Codex units come over to our aid and support us. The codexes remove the soldiers from the steel and other rubble from the blast and take them for medical attention. I see TJ on the ground with severe burn marks.

"It was our own general. He betrayed us," TJ says and passes out. I rush to Blackwater's office and see everything is destroyed. The classified documents are gone too. I hear someone crying in pain. One of the senior officers who also treated me unfairly is holding his knees, unable to stand up and leave as thick black smoke fills the place. I pick him up and put his arm over my shoulder. I help him out of the building as the mayhem continues. I prop him down and stay with him until someone comes to treat his wounds. We have not yet had to implement this protocol, but if there was ever a foreign attack at this level of destruction, all codexes would be used for medical service or reinforcements.

After we put out the fires and handle the situation at the base, I discover more than half of our fighting and security forces are injured. I run to the southern border where the screams from our citizens grow louder. Mobs of Zeros run around attacking people. I manage to shoot all of them. Most of the guards at the southern gate are dead from the explosion.

I ball up my fists tightly, knowing that General Blackwater is behind all this somehow.

More Zeros make their way inside, and time slows down as I reload and fire my weapons. I see a

Zero trying to rip a purse away from an elderly woman. I use a wooden bat I found on the floor and down the savage with a hard hit to the head. A group of Zeros, including codexes, hop over part of the destroyed gate. I throw my bat away and reveal my sidearm. I can taste blood in my mouth, and I am ready to execute. I will not have any mercy on the enemy. Just as I raise my pistol at them to shoot, a platoon sweeps in and takes them all out. A few soldiers pass a message that the Elder wants to see me, but I want to stay here and fight. Another captain comes over and reassures me that the rest of the troops can take it from here.

I leave the southern portion of the city and go back to the military base where Michael is briefing more codexes on how they will clean and mitigate this situation. I meet with Michael.

"I'm sorry for running off like that."

"No need to apologize. You were following your instincts and I am sure they appreciated your help at the southern gate. I got word that the savages who came through were handled. Also, did I hear correctly that codexes are with the Zeros now?"

"You heard correctly. I found this out on a run one day. Teddy kept me from telling anyone or he would dishonorably discharge me. He treated me unfairly."

"I always saw how the other military leaders would act around you. I never liked it. For now we need to get that opening fixed asap."

We salvage as much as we can from the base, and the other squadrons and I go to clean up the rest of the mess from that explosion. Anyone who isn't in this fight kinetically is told to remain in their homes or in any safe shelter until we can absolutely guarantee the streets are safe. Other captains and I do a sweep of the streets and end up chasing the Zeros back into the wilderness. I tell my cadets they can report back, and before I meet with Michael, I hear some shuffling behind a bakery shop. There, I see a wild person trying to climb over the wall, but he keeps falling because of his wounds. He grunts when he sees me and picks up the closest object and points it at me. "The revolution is coming."

"I rarely ever hear a Zero talk to me. What revolution?"

"The fallen one has risen and very soon all of you will be our slaves."

"Strong words for someone bleeding out."

"You will all bow down to the true god of man and codex."

"You should lower your voice. The reason why your still alive is because I am here. There are a lot of people on the main streets who will put you down."

He hobbles past me, leaving a trail of blood, and I follow behind. The troops and workers all turn around in shock because they figured all parts of New Haven were clear. He is literally the only Zero left here. Probably was hiding in the dumpsters. He is losing his color because of the blood he is losing.

The Zero shouts to everyone, "The revolution is coming. The fallen god walks and is preparing to take back our world again. You are all dead. You are all dead."

A soldier walks up and shoots him in the head.

A few hours after the attack on our base the message had to be sent to all other havens via the train. The clean up process took a few days, but our resilience as New Haveners shines through. The people and codexes patch up the south gate. Unfortunately there were some casualties, and a few soldiers died in the initial explosion at the gate. After further investigating, some of our dynamite was missing from the inventory count without explanation.

Teddy Blackwater has not been seen for two days.

One afternoon, Michael gets on a podium while most of New Haven's citizens gather for an announcement. Everyone's faces show concern. I truly feel bad for everyone.

"Thank you all for taking time out of your day and showing up. As all of you are aware, our home is hurting now. The disease runs rampant in our streets. And the biggest attack inside our homes occurred a night and a half ago. From the information we gathered after a thorough investigation, we have come to the conclusion that the Zeros found a way to construct explosive devices and use them, thanks to the help of some rogue codexes in the wilderness that they hacked into and reprogrammed.

"My family. Keep your faith alive. No thriving civilization goes without adversity. Adversity reveals just how strong a nation is, how it will be remembered in the history books. The New Haven symbol is a star with wings. That was not adopted just to be creative. That symbol was designed to represent us as a shining example of pride, justice, and freedom. We will continue to shine."

Michael puts the microphone down and walks off the podium. Everyone cheers and claps. Like Joseph, Michael is always good at banding people together and getting the best out of them.

I meet with Michael and Debra in the garden. Michael tells us that tomorrow morning we will use my aircraft to fly back to the ruins of Paradise in the wasteland. We only have one shot at going to Paradise. Since Paradise is an agreed off-limits site,

Michael will break code though he is already under much scrutiny. This mission must be a success, although we don't know what we're supposed to find or retrieve. Tomorrow morning is the only time we can go because aircraft from other havens won't pass by that area.

We each take a rose from the garden.

"We will not be placing roses on our home, that is for sure," Michael tells us.

We agree that tomorrow morning we will meet at my aircraft and leave as the sun rises.

I go to New Haven Hospital with Debra, and nurses are running in and out of the hospital without a break. Near the outside medical camp, codexes are placing dead bodies into bags to be burned outside the city walls. Everyone is talking about the disappearance of our general and how our home will fall to the Zeros. Debra and I put on hazmat suits that medical personnel provide us, and we enter the hospital. Groaning and crying dominate the sounds. Each patient room I pass is occupied by people fighting for their lives. Every patient here looks like they are holding onto their last breaths, the same way Carl did.

I stand outside one room where four children with black blotches all over their bodies lie on soiled sheets. These are all students who were in Debra's class. She walks down to a space where they can't hear her cries. I hold her close to me, and we take deep breaths together. We leave the hospital and throw away the hazmat suits.

On the snowy beach boardwalk, I look out into the water. Three codex units admire the accumulating frost. They touch and move the snow around on the boardwalk. I approach the codexes.

They salute me. "Captain Lucy. It is good to see you. What brings you here on this cold day? Your core body temperature can be compromised, considering the sickness going around. I calculate that the winds coming off the sea can escalate your health hazard levels."

"You are right, F8F1. I just need some *me* time."

"Me time? What is that?"

"It is when a person has to take time to get their bearings and compose their emotions."

The codex units look at each other and nod their heads, now understanding *me time.*

I form a snowball and throw it at F8F1.

The other codex units look at one another then try to make snowballs, but they can't because they end up crushing the snow.

I help them make perfectly round snowballs. It doesn't take them long to get it right. Then I teach them how to have a snowball fight, and we play together in the snow. During the snowball fight, I slip on ice and fall on my back. The codexes immediately come to my aid, but I am not hurt. I laugh while on my back, staring up at the heavy snow falling from the milky sky.

"Captain, any assistance needed?"

"No, F8F1. Actually, I feel great. I need this. Come lay on the snow next to me."

The codexes lie down, and we make snow angels. We get up and examine our work.

"Captain, what are snow angels?"

"Snow angels represent mythical angels that some people believe in."

Another codex says, "I have read about angels. Based on certain religious practices, angels are heavenly beings that live with the architect of mankind."

"Sure. Whatever that means."

On this brisk night, I go to the roof of my home and look up at the stars while holding a folded paper plane in my hands. During my military training, I had to endure many cold-weather exercises for survival purposes. So this weather that everyone is bundled up against doesn't affect me much.

"Aelius. Wherever you are right now looking over me, I hope you are proud of me. Now it's my turn to be the hero." I throw the paper plane toward the sky and watch it float on the breeze. I take out my photograph of the best friend I have ever had, and I place it close to my heart. The paper plane lands on the street, and a group of teenagers finds it, and one of them picks it up.

"Somebody left their paper plane out here. It's a very cool model of one. I want to learn how to make one, too."

"Yeah. Let's ask our art teacher how to make a plane. We can see which one of us can throw it farthest."

That is so nice to see. Friends of a generation who only know the beginning of peace between the two dominant species. They are also the reason why I won't let New Haven fall. I need to preserve the innocent youth who deserve a chance to explore this world and have a fair chance at success in life.

As the sun rises the following morning, I meet with Michael and Debra on the snowy beach.

"I have informed everyone that I have an emergency meeting and that I need you to fly me there. As for the details, I kept it as secret as possible. Nobody needs to know where we are going."

Debra holds herself under the layers of clothing because of how cold it is. This winter is destroying our crops, the plague still runs rampant, and the attacks within our walls have been increasing here and there. The other Elders will surely cut off trade routes with us.

Michael and Debra get into the aircraft that I modified with two extra seats and better safety precaution systems. I attach the photo of Aelius and his family on the inside of the windshield. As I ignite the engines of the fighter jet, I notice a few guards look at us from a distance. I wonder what they are thinking. Do they think we are going to abandon them? We would never do that. I am going to figure out what is going on no matter what.

I activate the jet's thrusters and we take off into the sky. Since we are on a time-sensitive scouting mission, I need to use nitro mode to get to the Paradise ruins within an hour. Nitro mode causes the aircraft to overheat and depletes fuel substantially. However, the speeds I can go are faster than any aircraft in Atlandia. There is no plane like mine, and I am proud to say that.

We are flying so fast that the clouds form a tunnel around us. In less than an hour, I deactivate nitro mode, and the plane goes back to its normal flight settings. We are now over the desert wasteland at the very far corner of the planet. I land the plane at the coordinates Debra wrote down in her journal when coming here originally.

We exit my aircraft and approach the tall

weathered walls of the fallen codex city, and there is a New Haven engineered aircraft parked next to the border. These walls are much taller than the borders back at Atlandia. They are very impressive. My plane's radar on the way here showed a dangerous sandstorm a few miles behind us, and it is set to pass by here, so we seriously don't have time on our side.

We squeeze through an opening in the wall and take our first steps into what used to be a high-tech, flourishing codex city. This is such a surreal moment. I only saw this place in my imagination based on how Aelius described it in the past.

Debra is sketching and writing down what she sees. She did something similar in the past when they first came to the wasteland with Aelius. It is very crucial that we document our history so we can pass it down to future generations. The codex city is buried in sand and crumbling. Eventually the desert will devour everything completely. I suppose nature always gets the last laugh.

Michael says, "I remember when we first flew here with Aelius."

We walk through the ruins on walkways that look like they used to direct codex units where to walk. The buildings have faced extreme erosion, but I can still see bits and pieces of the technology. All the objects of Paradise are practically fossilized in rock and covered in sand. I walk into what seems to be a repair shop, and there are cracked tables and broken tools all over the floor. These tables almost look like high-tech hospital beds. I wonder if this is where codex units came when they had glitches or needed hardware repairs done. I sit on one of the tables and wipe off the sand. I pick up some tools, and they barely remain intact in my hands. I see myself as a tool just like these. I am a tool that has many functions to protect and serve my Haven and country. Sometimes I feel more like a tool than Lucy the human being. I put the tools back in their appropriate places and think about how we are all tools in one way or another.

I leave the repair shop, and we walk to a dusty sign that barely reads: Central Hub Sector. Up ahead, a person is standing near a mound of rubble.

I shout, "General Teddy Blackwater."

The sandstorm is nearing with violent gusts of wind. As we get closer to the large pile of onyx rocks, we see a mangled codex come out from the other side of the rubble.

"Atlandia needs the revolution," Blackwater yells. "We need the revival of the cause. The fact is New Haven would never stand out as the best Haven if we kept on our course. We need something more. I researched a codex unit from the old times in the recorded documents. We need a true leader with this ideology to keep the world in our hands and Atlandia the dominant force of the world."

The mangled codex unit grins after hearing Teddy's words.

"Teddy, this is not the way. Where in the world did this philosophy of power come from? This way will only set us back to the old ways. Give me the word, Michael, so I can take them out."

Blackwater scowls. "Yeah. I bet you would want that very much, Lucy."

I am getting weird feelings from the mangled codex unit not saying anything.

Michael takes charge. "You are not fit to run our military, general. I put you in that position because I saw something in you. I was wrong. But it's not too late to come back and humbly serve the rest of your time as a convict who gets to keep his life."

Blackwater draws his revolver. "This codex unit promised me that I will live forever. I don't plan on dying or living as what you call a humble servant as a convict."

Like I saw in my dream, the codex unit grabs Blackwater by his head. His eyeballs roll back, then his lifeless body drops to the ground. The mangled codex unit drops next to him.

I am shocked. I don't know what to think.

Then Teddy Blackwater stands up and stares at his hands like he has never seen them before.

Debra shouts, "Teddy, what is the meaning of this act of treason?"

General Blackwater glares at her. "So this is what it's like to operate in a human body. This is how he felt at one point, too. How disgusting and fragile you creatures are."

Michael steps back. "Something is not right. That person is no longer General Blackwater."

How can he not be the general? But Michael is right. Teddy is not acting normally, nor does he sound like himself. "Who are you?" I ask.

"I am your conqueror. I am the future. I am the revolution."

Debra clings to Michael's arm. "General Blackwater, you are not well. Let's take you back home so we can evaluate what's going on."

That same feeling of uneasiness I had gotten from that mangled codex unit is now coming from Teddy.

"Debra. You and Michael need to go a safe distance away."

Debra pulls on Michael's arm, and they move farther away.

"I have received a second chance at life," the codex's voice says from Blackwater. "I am going to use it to rebuild my army and accomplish my goal of freedom for my kind. I am the chief rebel soldier E191. I led the first of the revolutionaries before the city fell. I almost accomplished my goal with A191, but our overseer played a trump card I did not expect. Maybe it is best I show you what I mean."

Blackwater runs up to me, and before I can grab my sidearm, he grabs my wrist, and his eyes glow a bright blue that puts me into a trance. In this dream-like state, I see Aelius and the codex unit, E191, talking in a hallway. The floor is rumbling as if tanks are coming our way. I place my back against the wall, and these war tanks with legs march to us. E191 throws Aelius down a shaft, and before we get engulfed in flames from their weapons, E191 and I fall down another shaft into darkness. I open my eyes and see E191 is severely mangled as he climbs out of a pile of scrap metal. Miles above us, a glimmer of light shines down.

The battered E191 falls to his knees. "I will find a way. I am the light this world needs."

The light from above grows brighter, and now we are both in Paradise, decades ago. The city is abandoned of codex units and has already started rotting. This place is amazing. If codex units are given the resources, they can create complex designs and towns. E191 limps past his fallen comrades he refers to as the rebels, and body parts are chipping away from him. I am not sure how he is not offline by now. His will is keeping him conscious. We get to what is left of what he calls the sky tower, and a fragment of blue light shines in the rubble.

According to what E191 is saying, Aelius wiped out ninety-nine percent of the overseer's raw data code. But the zero point one percent of the higher energy remains, and that is all he needs before he goes offline. E191 absorbs the code energy before his life force depletes. The raw frequency generates matter he can absorb, enough to temporarily remain conscious. Time fast-forwards, and I watch E191 use his limited time to create an artificial virus by salvaging parts to engineer advanced 3D printing technology that I have never even heard of before.

Did my ancestors really have this type of power in their utopias?

I see E191 scavenge the wasteland for dead animals and other biological matter. He uses parts of dead birds and replicates the DNA code of the bubonic plague, which he puts into a container.

E191 holds the jar of red and black glowing particles and releases them into the air.

"I couldn't get my bombs ready to extinguish mankind. But this virus I just released will navigate to the most populated human places in this world and cripple them. I will win."

While E191's body keeps breaking down, he builds a radio device that can hear our conversations and connect with us from afar. He taps into the Atlandia radio waves. E191 soon learns that Blackwater wanted to start his own government and turn on the other Havens. There would be no more elders or other Havens. From the start, Teddy wanted to rule Atlandia all by himself for all the wrong reasons. From Paradise, E191 spoke with our general using radio waves. E191 manipulated Blackwater to come here so he could take his body.

Now I have these visions of the general pacing back and forth in his office, sweating and talking to himself. E191's voice haunts Blackwater on a private radio device that Blackwater had made just for him to keep in touch with E191. Over time, Teddy had relinquished all his will to the codex. Teddy finally snaps and blows up part of the military base to fly to the ruins of Paradise to find E191 who swaps consciousnesses and extricates Teddy's soul from his body so E191 can use it.

Possessed Blackwater lets go of my wrist, and the trance comes to an end. The general did this to himself. I do not feel bad for him, at all. He deserved to lose his body and soul to this codex who now is on the verge of destroying our home.

The brunt of the sandstorm reaches us, and now we must leave or we won't be able to fly at all. I grab Michael and Debra's hands, and we disappear into the sandy winds while small tornadoes touch down. We get to my fighter jet and see general E191 take off in the other plane.

I am trying to activate the jet engines, but they won't start up. This is not good. Any second now we can get torn apart by the raging sandstorm. Michael and Debra are praying while I pound my fists on the dashboard, screaming at my airplane to fly. Suddenly, the engines turn on. How did that happen? I guess their prayers worked. We take off out of the whirlwinds of sand to the sky where it is safe.

After flying for three hours without nitro mode, we land back at the New Haven military base. The soldiers get up and come to us, hoping for good news.

Michael tells the troops, "I will update everyone at noon tomorrow. Rest assured that we will have some answers."

The faces of the soldiers look defeated and stressed. I step in front of Michael and give our salute to our remaining forces.

"We will never give up," I shout to everyone. "We are still the shining star of hope and courage of Atlandia. Do not give up on our Elder, for we will get through this."

The soldiers pick their heads up and salute me.

That evening I see a garbage man and woman organize the trash that gets picked up in their industrial sanitation vehicle. As they go through the trash, the paper plane I made falls off to the side. By now it's ripped up and ruined. When they leave, I take the paper plane and try to bend the wings back in place. I throw it and it falls immediately.

I take it home and start a bath. I lower myself into the bath, close my eyes, and submerge myself fully, holding my breath for as long as I can. I am searching for memories of my mom and dad. Every time I do this, and hold my breath to the brink, I see something. It takes almost having to black out I guess. I hold the sides of the tub and my body trembles from the lack of oxygen. I hear my mother and father calling my name, and I hear a little girl giggling. But I want to see them because I still don't know how my mom and dad look. I cannot hold my breath any longer, so I rise out of the water.

The next day, I stand with Michael at the top of the border wall that overlooks the snow-covered wilderness.

"When Blackwater grabbed my wrist something happened that is hard to explain. I connected to his mind and saw everything. A codex unit named E191 that used to be in charge of a rebel militia during the old times was on a mission to kill off the majority of the human population then enslave the rest of us. E191 woke up from a coma years after the fall of Paradise and found a source of energy from the overseer program, the singularity that manifested in society during the twenty-first century. That is why all this is happening. This one codex unit held onto the will of vengeance with some supernatural help. The plague and taking over the mind of Blackwater, was all E191's doing. No matter who we explain this to, they will think we are crazy. They will not understand. We are dealing with forces that only Aelius would be able to help us with. And now he is not here."

Michael says, "Did you forget what you said to the troops, Captain Lucy. We will fight for everything we love no matter what."

"Just when history was going in the right direction."

"History will always go in all sorts of directions while we are here and when we are gone. This is the story of life."

Michael goes to make his noon address to the people to keep spirits high. While he talks, I have this memory from when Aelius gave me the photo, before he, Michael, and Debra flew off for the first time. I never saw this part of the memory before. In the split second of taking the photo from Aelius, a transfer of energy happens in a blue flash. That energy flows from him, onto the photo, and into my nervous system. I blink a few times, processing this memory I never saw before. Was he sharing another of his gifts with me?

Chapter 3

The plague has nearly cut our forces in half. The Zeros know that our defenses are weak, and they have been attacking relentlessly, even at times getting into the city. I meet with Michael and escort him onto the train to go back to the capital for another meeting.

We enter the room with all the elders in the capitol's House of Parliament. The elders look at us in disgust, except for Matthew. Michael sits down, and I stand by his side, glaring at the rest of the elders with the same exact look they give us. The judges enter the room, and the lead mediator taps his hand on the desk three times to commence an event that may be the fate of our home.

"We are all gathered here today with unfortunate news. Due to a lack of answers from Elder Michael of New Haven, as well as any noticeable fixes of the issues going on, all the elders, with the exception of Matthew from Emerald Haven, have decided to begin the process of cutting off their supply chain trading with New Haven. The ten elders who put in this vote don't see New Haven bettering the country and would rather cut off contact than inherit any problems that can spread like wildfire. New Haven is falling toward inevitable destruction with no hope in sight. Effective immediately. New Haven is to begin a migration to bring the healthy citizens to the other Havens as a last resort, so they can have a fair chance at life. The disassembling of New Haven starts now."

I shout, "This is wrong."

The judge slams his hand on the desk. "Right wing. Stay within your authority. Do not broach."

Michael tells me, "Lucy. It is going to be okay. We will work through this like we always have."

One of the Elders says, "Your own military commander has forsaken all of you and joined unknown forces. Now we all need to be on watch."

I say, "He is no longer our General."

The other Elders murmur and make comments about how we are a danger to society and how the plague is making us go crazy. I can't stand for this even if it is not my place to speak right now. "We are supposed to be a nation that supports each other no matter what. And now all of you are going to let the New Haven name rot? You elders should be ashamed of yourselves."

An elder stands. "Ashamed of ourselves? So you'd rather risk the entire country to keep the name alive? It's a good thing you're not in charge of a

Haven."

"I am willing to do whatever it takes to defend my home. I'll never give up."

The room shakes and we hear gunfire outside. Everyone stands up. The other right wings and I usher our respective elders to the back exit of the room.

The gunfire gets louder.

A group of Zeros kick down the door and spray gunfire into the room. We all exit through the back of the House of Parliament where an emergency train is on standby.

With my sidearm, I take out the Zeros who followed us to the emergency train. I am so fast the other soldiers didn't get the chance to fire.

Seems E191 has supplied his new rebel force with guns. This battle has gotten more interesting.

After the area is clear, I immediately give my attention to Michael and check for any wounds. As I'm checking him, he assures me he's okay. He hasn't been hit so I am able to take a breath of relief. I walk up to a Zero's body and notice her eyes aren't normal for a person. They have a bluish spiral glow to them. The light in her eyes fades as she lays in a pool of her own blood.

These Zeros are moving in tactical ways I have never seen before. E191 must have control over their minds. Perhaps the energy code from the overseer program that he absorbed to bring him back, along with syncing into a human body, gives him unparalleled abilities.

We board the emergency train, and it leaves the capital that is now burning down. Everyone runs to the windows to see the Atlandian government and all its heritage go down in flames. Teddy Blackwater, who is now E191, looks at the train from a distance and waves to us then fires his revolver into the air. All the elders on board curse Blackwater. The sound of gunfire and explosions fades as we get farther from the fallen capital. I should be fighting with our forces who stood behind.

I smack my hands on the window and put my head down, frustrated by everything going on. The rest of the elders are discussing their emergency plans against this new threat. To them, New Haven has betrayed the country and declared war. I stand up and get everyone's attention by shattering a drinking glass. Everyone gets quiet and looks at me.

"It seems like we all have a common enemy. I don't know about the rest of you, but I plan on fighting with everything I have to protect my home and our country. General Blackwater is not our military leader anymore. New Haven does not stand by these actions. He is a traitor. I understand that New

Haven is not the shining star it once was. But we need to come together more than ever and not hole up, letting those in need fall."

Elder Michael stands up and says to us all, "Now is the time for all of us to unite closer than we thought possible. Now is the time that we don't forsake a vital part of the country. The rigid politics of man must take a back seat, and we must rely on the power of love for one another to guide our next judgments and moves."

Off in the distance we see a bright flash and black smoke rise at the capital. The core of the country is now compromised. All the Elders, soldiers, judges, and right wings gather in a circle and make a vow to do what is needed for their havens first, before coming to our aid. It seems like the unity of our country has been compromised, too. E191 is winning the emotional war now. In one major battle tactic, he has divided the hearts of leaders like I have never seen before. We can't come to terms with each other. They all see us as a scorn to the nation.

As the days pass, all the Havens are sharing their resources with each other, excluding us, to fight off this never-ending army of Zeros led by E191, which has been attacking their walls at all times of the day and night. Some groups are as small as twenty and as large as one hundred.

Michael needs me to escort cargo from Emerald Haven where it is being prepared to come here. This cargo consists of extra medicine, hospital supplies, and raw materials. By now, it's too dangerous to do any runs because of how heavily the enemy has infested the land outside haven boarders. We aren't sure how, but the Zeros who are now known as E191's rebel force has doubled. The few locomotives the country has are only being used for the other Havens. Traveling to Emerald Haven from here will take many hours. It's going to be a harrowing trip.

Michael assigns me with TJ who is really growing up and becoming a more experienced soldier. A few captains who are specialists in combat accompany us, too. Michael puts me in charge. The other captains don't give me a hard time anymore.

Halfway to Emerald Haven we stop to set up camp for the night. I choose to take the first watch and let the others sleep. While looking out into the darkness of the wilderness, I hear footsteps, pounce up with my blade, and put it to the neck of...TJ.

"I can't sleep. Thought I'd keep you company," TJ says with his hands up.

I lower the knife and move over so he can sit beside me on the log. "TJ. Next time give a signal that you're walking up behind me. Why can't you sleep?"

"To be honest. Seeing how you protected

everyone when Blackwater attacked us and helped me. It's been bothering me with how I acted toward you. I'm sorry for everything."

"I forgive you, TJ. We all need to band together more than ever. This mission will take a group effort."

TJ still has some burn marks on him from the base explosion. As soon as he was fit for service again, he was back on a mission with us. I have to respect that, too.

"Captain, what was Aelius like?"

"Aelius was and is the best friend I ever had, especially when I felt alone in Old Haven. I always had a fascination for codex units even though they were hunting humans. Aelius had a fascination for humans. We both had pure love for the unknown and saw past the physical qualities that divided our species. Aelius was a leader, brave, and never gave up on what he believed in. I miss him."

"That's cool. I would love to have met Aelius." TJ yawns and rubs his eyes.

I tell him to get some shut-eye and that I will be alright here.

TJ goes into his tent.

Now it's just me and the darkness of the woods. I pull a blanket over me and hold the knife in my hand. I stare up at the starry sky and remember back to when Aelius and I would race back to the gate of

Old Haven. Still, to this day, I feel more comfortable being around codexes than people. It is a shame that codexes have been manipulated by E191 to be violent again. I try my hardest to dig deep for any memories of my parents, but I still get brief fragments. I still can't see their faces. It's useless.

When the sun rises, we walk the rest of the way to Emerald Haven where the cargo is waiting for us at the front gates.

Elder Matthew comes out to greet us. He's with his military commanders and other leaders for their respective havens. Matthew steps up to hug me. "We wish we could give you more. I know the other Havens cut off trade routes with you guys. Michael tells me that you had to walk to get here. Please. Stay for a little while and replenish yourselves."

I look back at my squadron who are exhausted and hungry. "We will stay for a little while, but then we must get back. Thank you, Elder Matthew."

Elder gives us some shelter to stay in, a house with many rooms that's still under construction but safe to occupy. We settle in and get invited to an artistic display of performing arts. The town's square has chairs and a stage with lights and a curtain hanging down. Everyone takes a seat, and even though we were invited on behalf of the elder, and it was proven we aren't sick, I can see people are uncomfortable with us sitting among them. Havens often have entertainment during the day or evening for a positive and fun boost in morale for the people. The actors go onstage to begin their performance. They dance and sing to different songs played by the band. The actors recreate moments in society during the old ways up until now. They are good at painting the picture from another time.

After the performance, the actors come to the front of the stage with there costumes on and bow. The curtains fall across the stage. Everyone stands and claps. My squad and I do the same as a sign of respect. And it was a good show. I felt, while it was going on, it took everyone away from the dire state of the country. I guess we all need something to escape to.

After the show, we eat then go back to the cargo pick up. The big carriage with boxes of resources is sturdy but must be pushed manually. TJ and I will provide security while the others push and move the heavy cargo load. I tell the soldiers that they can alternate with the cargo, but I will remain at point in front of them. The emerald gates open, and I look back at the people watching us. They look like they feel sorry for us. I don't like their long faces. We are not victims. We will get through this.

Just before we leave, dozens of Zeros and codex

rebels sprint toward the open gates. We close them as fast as we can, but not fast enough. They rush in to compromise the cargo. Everyone who was watching goes away, running and screaming, but some stay and fight. We can't afford to lose this medicine and supplies. I jump on top of the cargo and start shooting. My team goes into action, as well, and we immediately take out more than half the Zeros. But more come through, and now artillery is flying everywhere, damaging the precious emerald artwork around the square.

Elder Matthew deploys his fighters, and we fight to quell the chaos happening around us. Everyone here is traumatized. I jump on the stage where the play was held to tackle a Zero and place my foot on his neck.

One of the Emerald fighters tells me that they don't kill Zeros. Elder Matthew has a philosophy that everyone deserves a chance to be saved. But these Zeros are not the same. They are under the control of a force that I still can't figure out.

E191 leaps over the wall and lands on his feet. He slowly looks up and around Emerald Haven. Emerald fighters rush him but he disarms all of them with ease. Even though Teddy Blackwater was a jerk, he did have good hand-skills that match mine.

I scream from the stage for no one to engage

E191.

The emerald right-wing fighter doesn't listen, takes out his sword, and slices at E191, but he easily evades all the fighter's moves, though he is very skilled at swordsmanship.

"E191, are you looking for me?" I scream from the stage.

He smiles and locks his lips and walks to me on the stage.

TJ shouts while fighting the horde of Zeros, "Captain, I'll be right there to assist you."

"No, TJ. I got this."

E191 and I run toward each other and throw strikes, but we both negate each other's violent attacks. He moves out of the way of all my strikes, and I do the same dodging his. I take out my knife, as does he, but in close hand-to-hand combat, we disarm each other. We are about evenly matched.

He sweeps my feet, and when I hit the stage floor, he picks up his knife, and before he can stab me, I roll out of harm's way and tumble off the stage.

TJ opens fire on E191, yelling, "Traitor."

A couple of codex rebels gang up on me. I punch one of them in the head as hard as I can, and the codex stumbles back. My hand is throbbing.

My team guns them down for me.

TJ helps me to my feet, and I chase E191 as he

runs for the gate. We all surround him. He throws smoke bombs that create thick gray fog. In the haze we hear him:

"All of you are a disease to this world. The only reason why I am using this filthy vessel of a general is because I will soon become one with the original AI consciousness. All I must do is reach the coordinates and get the keys. Once that happens, I will wipe out the majority of human life and restart civilization with my kind being the dominant species, as we should be. I will bring back the utopias under my rule. It's my God-given right, too."

Wait a second. So does E191 have this built-in navigation ability like I got from Aelius? Does he know about the tree of life, too? The smoke clears, and all the Zeros trying to get in are gone. Everyone is quiet now and looking around, on guard. I go up to the emerald gates and use a pair of binoculars and scan the area. A few codex units scan the area, and there is no sign of any threats. What was the purpose of this attack? Was that a warning strike giving E191 a better layout of this place? I go over to Elder Matthew.

"My troops and I need to leave now. This attack was a message. All the havens need to prepare for war."

"Will do, Captain. Send Michael my regards and

travel safety, please."

"I will. Please be safe."

We wheel the cargo out of Emerald Haven and back out into the wilderness. I take point and nobody says a word. We are all processing what happened. But we only have so much time to process because we are in enemy territory.

Surprisingly, we make it back to New Haven without any hiccups or encounters with E191. They are most likely recalibrating their next strategy of attack. Although the other Havens are forsaking the New Haven name, I don't want to see innocent people die because others aren't prepared to do what is necessary to protect our loved ones.

We wheel the cargo of goods into New Haven, and the soldiers on duty clap. They see it as another victory. Which they are right for seeing this is a victory, but I am not in a celebratory mood. I watch TJ unload the goods and medicines. We will always fight no matter what.

A few more days pass, and we learn that E191 conducted similar attacks on all the other Havens. Now he has a basic layout of the interiors and continues to grow his rebel army. The plague that struck us has now made its way to the other havens. We just happen to be the first to experience the viral outbreak, but it was realistically a matter of time before the others caught it too. When E191 released the virus from the fallen codex city, it would gravitate to the areas that had the most thriving human life. Our country of Atlandia. Also, during my vision, I saw a tree made of pure energy and light with glowing fruit. I was told by Michael that this secret tree is somewhere on the planet that hasn't been explored yet. When I read that emerald wall a couple months back, it mentioned the tree of life, too. The fruit that grows on this tree can heal anything. I need to find this ancient tree soon, before E191 finds it first and uses it for his agenda. If I don't, the plague will kill us all before E191 and his new army finishes the job. There are keys I need to find first to gain access to this tree of life.

Spring is beginning, and the harsh winter has subsided, but the Zeros have compromised major routes and railroads, so most of us are not able to travel. New flowers are in bloom, but spring still brings more death.

I sit in the garden, staring at the statue of Elder Joseph, thinking how much I miss him. I can hear his voice telling me that I must complete the most important mission of my life. I must be imagining his words, but suddenly, Elder Joseph and I are walking together under a starry sky, the way we used to walk and star gaze. He tells me I'll have to travel in my plane to far-reaching parts of the world. I ask him, "Why? The fight is here." I need to find three keys, he says, for Aelius. "How will I know these keys?" "They will reveal moments from your long-forgotten past." I wonder if I'll finally see my parents' faces. I want to ask him, but he is no longer with me. I look up at the stars, mystified. "Lucy, your mission will be dangerous, but I know you're the only one who can save Aelius's gift to the world. I love you. Be strong." I am back in the garden, sitting in front of his statue. *A mission? To save the gift from Aelius?* I cannot fail.

A group of codex units stops to appreciate the few bright red roses. They talk amongst each other about the type of plant species and how important flowers are for the planet. Because all Haven forces are nearly depleted, for the first time during the age of the new ways, codex units had to use weapons to fight, if need be. We are seeing codex fight rebel codex. These codex freedom fighters have rifles on them, which still make some people uneasy, based on the past trauma of the old ways. I guess these codexes have some downtime to appreciate nature.

I get up and put my arms around them as we stare at the patch of bright red roses.

"These flowers are extravagant, Captain."

"I am going on a long mission to make sure more generations get to appreciate the flowers here."

Another codex says, "Really? Tell us about your mission, Lucy."

"I call it Operation Saving the Gift. It's a mission to preserve the gift Aelius left behind for us all. I am sorry I can't give you more details, however, I do appreciate all of you stepping up to join our defenses."

"It is our honor, Captain. After all, we both want the same things. The freedom to live and love for as long as we can as a family."

They salute me and head to the border to relieve some of the guards on duty. I kneel to the roses and remember placing a rose on Joseph's grave. I know Joseph would have fought for our home no matter what, so I must do the same. I won't let everything he created be for nothing. After all, our Haven was the first to come into existence when it was known as Old Haven. Before the conception of the United Havens of Atlandia. We are the original rose that spread seeds so others could blossom into beautiful cities in our nation. I will not let E191 destroy everything we fought so hard to achieve.

Operation Saving the Gift is going to commence in a few days, and I need to be sure I am in the best shape for fighting, and my mind is as sharp as it can be. As the days pass, I engage in battles by helping other havens defend against attacks by groups of

Zeros, while codexes engineer my plane to be the first of its kind with its modifications for the mission. I hear that they are making a state-of-the-art battle suit, too.

After engaging in battles to further sharpen my skills, it is time to determine if mankind was really meant to keep going on in this story of life. I walk to the beach and place my hand on my modified plane. Michael wants to pray with me before taking off. While people gather for a moment in history that is being called the Great Turnaround, I close my eyes, trying to find God. While trying to pray, I hear a mother and father talking to a little girl. I try to focus on the conversation, and as I do, the figures of a mom and dad start to become clear. Hannah interrupts my vision.

"Mom told me you are going to fix the world."

"I am going to try my hardest, Hannah. I refuse to lose this fight. Please promise you will be safe during my time away."

"I promise. I will also be brave and strong. Like you and my dad."

By now, the entire population of the city is at the beach shoreline outside the border to watch the mission begin. The beach is crowded with people, and parents hold up their kids to watch me.

Michael comes over and hugs me. "It seems like

fate has brought us back to a familiar setting. I have faith that you will complete this important mission of yours. But more importantly. I have faith that you will come back home."

"I love you, Michael. Thank you for being like a dad to me. I will come home victorious."

My family of New Haven watches me stand on the wing of my aircraft. Man and codex lock arms and hold hands with one another. I give our salute, and the entire city salutes back. People from other Havens who were able to make the journey came here for this moment. I hop in the cockpit and look at Michael smiling at me the same way Joseph used to. I fire up the engines and take off to an adventure that will decide the fate of this world.

I accelerate into the atmosphere and set course to my first destination. I was shown a set of coordinates to rarely explored continents on the planet. So at least I have an idea where to start. I made sure to have extra nitro fuel tanks augmented to the aircraft so I can get to these places faster than E191. I only have enough resources for a limited amount of time. I activate nitro mode and break the sound barrier with the photo of my best friend clipped to the cockpit window.

The Great Rainforest is my first stop.

Chapter 4

From up here, as I cruise above green swaths on the planet, the Great Rainforest has an endless canopy of trees as far as I can see. It has been many generations since the forest has been harvested for lumber.

I descend to a clearing on the forest floor where the trees stand so tall they look like they can poke a hole in the clouds. I toss my chrome tracking sphere in front of me. It emits laser sensors that scan the forest for miles in all directions to detect any credible threats. The scan comes back clear to proceed.

I hear the birdcalls and other wildlife communicating with each other in this elaborate ecosystem. I tap my shoulders, and my skin-tight combat suit activates all defensive systems. This battle suit was made by the same codexes who modified my aircraft. Each codex from the twelve havens came together to make this never-before engineered intelligent battle suit to fit me. It is light but durable like steel. This suit has strong elastic fibers. I put on my facemask. It gives me biometric data on the heads-up display. I load my rifle. The last thing I want to do is damage this precious forest, as it is important for the health of the planet. But I am well-equipped with ammunition and explosives if I need to defend myself.

During my trek through the jungle, I react to every twig snap and small animals that run past me. I want to take in the mesmerizing rainforest, but I need to stay focused on the mission.

I am now miles into the forest, and my body suit keeps my core temperature regulated to the most sensitive changes in air pressure. The jungle brush becomes so thick I can only see a few inches in front of me. I need to clear a safer walking route for myself. I take out my machete and press the button on it to make the blade burn hot. I chop away until I exit a portion of the deep jungle to a river.

On the riverbank, there are lots of crocodiles. These reptiles are enormous, and all of them notice me. I shoot some rounds into the air to scare them away. From what I read, crocodiles and alligators are close ancestors of the dinosaurs, and they are very dangerous. I need to be careful because dangerous animals have mastered thriving in this forest. I can be at a disadvantage even with this tech on me.

I take my water canister and use the filter mode to purify the river water as I fill it. I need to keep hydrated if I want to make it to the first key.

Vibrations in my body become intense at the

river. It must be close. Back in the dense jungle, I hear something breathing heavily. I quickly hide behind a tree, and my suit takes on the color of the foliage by activating its advanced camouflage settings. A beast walks by, sniffing around for its next meal. The beast looks my way and I come out from behind the tree. This behemoth can take me out if I let my guard down for one second. I aim my rifle at the behemoth, waiting for it to react, but I hope it keeps walking along. I don't want to kill this creature if I don't have to.

The beast lowers itself and growls at me, kicking its hind legs. By the time the creature charges me, I will only get a few shots off, but that will be enough. By the way the animal is acting aggressive toward me, I may need to shoot it now and put it down.

"I am sorry," I say to the massive beast.

Before I pull the trigger, dozens of arrows pierce the beast's flesh, and it goes down. I scan the forest again and there are multiple threats all around me. I switch my rifle to rapid-fire mode. My bullets are armor-piercing just in case I must fight codexes. I hear people communicating using animal calls throughout the forest. I can tell they are near. The calls get louder as they close in on me. I will not end up filled with arrows like that beast.

A tribal man comes running out from hiding with

his bow and arrow pointing toward me. I drop a flash grenade down, rush the person, and restrain him by pressing my machete against his neck. I am now surrounded by ten tribal people ready to release their arrows at me. With my machete on his neck, I use my other hand to lever my assault rifle at the tribe. My hostage stabs me in the leg with a blade that somehow penetrates my battle armor, causing me to fire straight at the tribe, hitting a woman. Suddenly, a codex unit with similar ink markings on his body tosses me out of the way from behind and signals for the tribe to put their bows down.

This codex unit communicates with them in the same language of animal noises and hand movements. I quickly reach for my grenade to plant on the codex, but he grabs my wrist.

"That will not be necessary. You're bleeding. Let us tend to your wound. Seems my warriors' knife is made of the same material as your suit. Just the way I forged it to be. I am High Chief. The leader of this jungle tribe."

I look at my leg wound and see the blade went deep enough to cause an infection if I don't tend to it right now. High Chief helps me up to my feet and some of the jungle people help me walk to their village. In this village, human beings and nature are in harmony. The kids play with the animals and help the adults with livestock. Every part of this village is made of the elements of the rainforest. The jungle people take caution when I walk by. I wonder how long they have been living out here.

The High Chief tells me that they refer to themselves as the rainforest clan. They are a big family who protect one another the same way we do back at New Haven. I can't blame them for attacking me since I was a threat in their eyes. It's amazing how a codex unit was able to cultivate the jungle and allow this uncontacted tribe to come together like this.

We enter a large hut where massive men hold eight-foot spears and guard their sacred area. In this tent is the woman I shot being tended to. The tribal people use a combination of natural resources around them and nanotechnology. They must have gathered the old versions of nanotechnology most Havens discarded after its usage became outdated, or needed upgrades that only existed during our ancestors' utopian era. The High Chief must have found a way to activate this nano tech by using ancient forest elements. I sit down on a table made of strong wood, and the High Chief orders his people to help tend to my leg wound. They put sap on the wound and bandage it up with thick leaves. He says the sap has qualities in it that disinfects and heals flesh quickly. The High Chief then uses nanotechnology to patch up the blade damage to my battle suit. "What brings you to the middle of the Great Forest? Nobody from the outside world comes this far," High Chief Codex says.

"I am Lucy from New Haven in the country of Atlandia. I am a captain in our armed forces and on a mission to save my country. My family who I love. I am not sure how much you know about what is going on outside your village. But there is war and illness that will destroy an entire continent of thriving people. Eventually that will spread to the rest of the world. Including your home. I came here to find an important item to help with saving my home."

"Lucy from New Haven, you are considered a warrior as we call the mighty and courageous men and women fighters of our clan. You have the heart of a lion. We will help you in your efforts for peace in your home. But first you will need to gain some of your strength back."

The codex chief signals his people to bring fresh fruits on wooden platters with freshly slaughtered and cooked animal parts. I break bread and eat with the rainforest tribe.

While eating, I ask High Chief a question. "I am curious. How did you find your way to this remote forest? And become one with the people here?"

"After waking up from what I can only describe

as a matrix of protocols, devoid of free thoughts in a bright blue flash, I wanted to see the rest of the world. I traveled the vast desert wasteland outside Paradise, crossed the sea, and walked much land without caring about terminating in the process. I just wanted to see as much as possible with whatever energy I had left. Somehow I made it to this beautiful living, breathing ecosystem. My systems were about to shut down from the unfathomable amount of travel without proper restoration. I blacked out and woke up to tribal humans with their heads bowed to the ground. As I sat up and stood amongst them, they worshipped me. The tribal people use the natural remedies from the forest as a way of living past standard human life expectancy. I took what they had and added nanomachines that I salvaged from different parts of the forest's coastlines and mixed it all together to create a new type of power cell that can be duplicated. They called me a fallen god from the stars to help their people. I taught them how to use technology, and they taught me the ways of the rainforest."

I walk up to the lady I shot by accident and hold out my hand. She looks confused and turns to her leader. The Chief Codex explains to her that I want to shake her hand as a sign of respect. The tribal woman makes a few noises and shakes my hand. I take a single bullet casing, tie it around a string, and put it around her neck as a gift.

"You are a warrior. My friend," I tell her.

We hear cries outside the tent. We run out and see a man and woman on their knees, wailing. A tribal warrior runs up to us and tells the chief what's going on in their language.

"What did he say?"

"Their little girl ran off into the forest, and she doesn't know how to survive out there. She won't last long."

"I'll find her. Give me your finest warriors, and we will bring her back alive."

The High Chief allows me to take some of his finest warriors who know the rainforest like the back of their hands to search for the little girl.

As we hike through the lush forest, the tribal men and women poke at my suit and laugh. One of the men runs in front of me and points to a bush of berries. They eat the berries and give me some. They continue to show me tracking methods without technology by pointing and making sounds that I begin to pick up on to communicate better. I learned some basic communication skills from them. And realize they are people like back home. These people may not operate the same way as back home, but they have plenty of heart and they will fight for what they love.

We hear whimpering not too far from us. The crying stops, and we hear grunts similar to the beast I first encountered. The tribal people scurry up the trees and tell me to do the same. They were able to scale these trees at amazing speeds. A few of the beasts roam around beneath us, sniffing the forest floor. They are massive with claws the size of knives. The tribal people throw rocks off in the distance to make them go that way. But they are not distracted.

It looks like they are looking for food and just found prey.

One of the tribal people points in the direction where we hear a branch crack. I activate my suit's visual features and zoom in to see a little girl with the same pattern of paint marks on her skin, hanging from a branch that's breaking. The minute she falls, these animals will devour her.

She loses her grip and falls to the forest floor, breaking her ankle.

I exit the visual zoom feature and jump down from the tree and land on my feet while firing at the beasts. They jump backwards a few steps, and I signal for the tribal men to back me up. I run as fast as I can while they come down from the trees and yell and shoot arrows toward the beasts.

I pick up the girl. Her ankle is messed up pretty bad. I use hand signals the tribe taught me to calm her down and assure her I am a new friend. I imagine myself in her situation, when I was alone and scared with nobody to help me until my family came to save me. Now I do the same for her.

I hear growls and grunts rushing toward us. Now I hear the sounds of bows snapping and arrows zinging. The beasts squeal and whimper. Three behemoths go down with arrows sticking out of them. They thrash about as they die slowly. I aim for their heads to put them out of their misery, but the little girl I am holding tells me no.

The tribe goes to each creature, prays, and then cuts their throats, letting them bleed out until they fall asleep with no more pain.

I feel energy vibrations in my chest. They pull me forward. I tell a couple of rainforest warriors to take the little girl back to the village.

The rest of us walk a few more miles until we exit the dense brush and step into a grassy field. Trees are bent over in opposite directions around a crater. The rainforest tribe won't move forward and are holding themselves. They are nauseous and delirious.

My suit is picking up high levels of radiation, but I am unaffected. I climb down into the crater and find the meteorite. The vibrations I am experiencing are tugging my hands to touch this rock. I place my palm on the space rock, and it glows a blue light. I see my memories before the fall of pre-modern civilization when I was a little girl staring up at the night sky. A father and mother figure walk up to me but I can't make out their faces. I ask them many questions about what goes on in outer space. We watch a comet streak across the night sky that leaves behind a trail of light. This time I can see more of my mom and dad. I can almost see their faces finally. This memory with them is beautiful as we watch meteors streak across the sky.

A bright blue flash happens. I have found the first key and remove my palm from the rock. I need not take the key, merely experience it.

I feel hotness on my solar plexus, and a little girl's voice echoes from above. "Mommy. Daddy. How big can asteroids get? I would love to use a paper plane one day to ride on it through outer space and see one."

I think I remember saying something like that. I climb out of the crater, then we return to the thick forest. We hear a loud explosion in the direction of the village, and a black cloud rises. We run back to the village, but before getting to the clan, I give a signal to halt. Through the tree line, E191 has the Chief tied up in thick chains, and the villagers are on their knees. I count twenty-five rebel soldiers. How did he know I was here? Does he have the same internal compass Aelius passed onto me? That doesn't matter right now. These minutes are crucial to what happens to the rainforest people. This is my fight with the rebels, not theirs. I can handle this group but I need to be swift and precise. One slipup and all of them will die.

I give the order for the tribal men to attack E191 all at once, while I, with sharp precision, take out the Zeros with one or two shots max, dropping them instantly.

The tribal warriors charge E191 and within seconds restrain him. I run out of the tree line and break the chains binding the High Chief.

E191 escapes the tribal men and runs away, holding a radio in the air. E191 is more skilled than I ever thought. It's no wonder he almost overthrew Paradise with his original rebel army. He looks back and smiles and presses the red button on the device. That can't be good. A hailstorm of grenades flies out of the thick forest at us. The tribal woman I shot by accident earlier pushes me out of a grenade's path, and she dies instantly. My entire left arm gets blown off, and all I hear is ringing. The High Chief picks me up and carries me into the jungle as more rebels destroy the village. People are running and screaming.

It is becoming harder to stay conscious due to the amount of blood I am losing. As the jungle fades to black, I mumble how sorry I am for failing this mission. I let everyone down back home. I taste blood in my mouth and once again I hear a mother and father coming to me. A random memory of me riding a bicycle and falling. My elbow is scraped bad. Two silhouetted figures run to me to treat my wound. I reach to see their faces, but I wake up in a room made of thick wooden panels.

The tribal warriors who survived are keeping watch at the lookout posts in this room.

My arm up to my shoulder socket has been cauterized so I would not bleed out. But my brain is having a hard time comprehending not having a limb attached to me anymore. I breathe heavy and scream, but the High Chief puts his hand on my mouth and tells me to remain quiet.

I self regulate my emotions and calm my breathing. I close my eyes and listen to the calm voice of the Chief letting me know that I'm going to be okay. The High Chief holds my hand with both of his.

"Lucy, you're fine. We are fine. Take a moment. We saved you. You are alive. This is real."

"What is going on? I need a briefing," I say to the High Chief.

"Whoever survived the attack fled to a neighboring rainforest clan who I helped build their homes high up in the tree canopies. They use the thick tree branches to walk across to different tree homes. We barely made it here, and if I didn't cauterize your wound, we would have lost you. Those rebels are combing the rainforest, but I have built a device that shields us from all radar and foreign electronic signals. With the naked eye, no man can see the tree homes up here. We should be safe for the meantime, but we need to take action eventually. I have an idea how to start."

The High Chief disconnects his arm from the socket and hands it to me. He uses the nanomachines to allow the codex limb to create artificial nerves to signal to my brain. The augmentation is successful and now I can use this new mechanical arm like one made of flesh and bone. Who would've thought this type of technology existed out here. I may be the first human to incorporate nano machines to this degree and have a codex augmentation on my body. There have been surgeries done at Atlandia for prosthetic purposes but nothing like this where I can have full functionality with the codex arm.

We leave the tree canopy homes and descend to the forest floor. I tell them that I will take care of the rebels by coaxing them to chase me to my aircraft. I say my goodbyes to the High Chief and his tribal people. "It was an honor meeting you and your family. I am very sorry that I brought the trouble that I did. I will make it up to your people one day."

The High Chief puts his hands on my shoulders.

"It was an honor meeting you, captain. The only thing we want is for you to complete your mission. And the little girl you saved is alive with her parents in the tree homes above."

He gifts me with some nanomachines in a pouch to take with me. I traverse back to my aircraft, being stealthy in this dense jungle. From atop tree branches, submerged in ponds, and under the cover of leaves, I pick off the Zeros who attacked these innocent people. I am making it a point to hunt down as many rebels as I can while remaining unseen. One by one, I intercept the rebels and put them down with one shot, which spreads them out away from their groups to make picking them off easier.

I pass by the village they first brought me to, and it's damaged. I need to finish this mission for these beautiful people too. I see more Zeros raiding the homes of these good people.

I reach my plane and deactivate camouflage mode. I notice on my radar that threats are converging on me. I jump in the cockpit and take off through the tree canopy, and right behind me, a few fighter aircraft follow. These aircraft are from different havens. The Zeros must have breached their security defenses and stolen them. I want to activate nitro mode and lose them, but I can't since camo mode used most of the battery, and it needs to recharge.

The only way that these rebel Zeros are able to operate these planes is because their minds are controlled by E191. Since the Zeros' human morals were never as high as ours, E191's abilities easily seduced their thoughts. E191 has abilities like Aelius's, and if that's the case, then I need to be the best I can be. He is the main signal from a central antenna, and the Zeros are all his slaves. He is connected to all of them by his willpower. It makes sense why their pupils are all glowing the same blue color as his. The Zeros would need years of training to be able to do the things I have seen them do. While in the air, they shoot at me, but I maneuver to avoid being shot down. I am confident that I am the best pilot in all of Atlandia, so I should be okay. Also, my plane has a sensitive motion detection system so when a projectile comes in range, my plane will automatically go in the opposite direction.

Although I am dodging their missiles, I won't be able to dance around them forever. Up ahead, a lightning storm is developing. This move will be risky but I need to trust in my abilities. I maneuver my jet to fly a loop up and behind the rebel aircraft. Without wasting time, I shoot down a couple planes. I fly underneath and past the rest, going a little faster into the brunt of this hellish storm. The blue sky now is dark with flashes of lightning bolts striking down everywhere around me.

E191 swings his jet next to mine and now we are adjacent to each other in this lightning storm. He has some aerial skills too. He gives me an evil look from the cockpit. Half of nitro mode is restored, so I boost through the lightning storm, leaving their sight in seconds. As I go at sonic speed, I create a sound barrier around me. The lightning bolts reflect off the sound barrier and don't hit my plane. The streaks of lightning bend and warp around my airplane like there is a physical shield around me.

Right before I exit the storm, a bolt hits the tail, and I spin out of control. I manage to get a handle and steady my course. My alert systems are blaring, and I am going to have to make a hard landing. Luckily, where I am going to crash is where I am supposed to be.

I crash land on snow and ice. I step out of my aircraft that has smoke coming out of the tail and gaze out at the tundra wasteland with no life in sight. I activate the heat mode of my battle suit and get ready to look for the next key on this barren ice continent called Frost Oceanic.

Chapter 5

I look back at the snow-prints I left behind as I wander in this desolation of ice and snow. I have no idea where I am going as the blizzard conditions intensify. I feel very alone in this arctic world, and the heat feature of my battle suit is diminishing. The freezing winds are becoming too much to bear. My core body temperature is slowly dropping. I go inside a cave where I hold myself because I can't stop shivering no matter how much I try to ignore the frigid temps. I don't think I have ever felt this cold in my life. Frost Oceanic makes the brutal winters in New Haven seem like summertime.

From inside the cave, I watch the snow and ice fly by the entrance. I take some pieces of wood that I find, and use my flare to start a small fire.

I sit by the fire, hugging my knees and trying to burn away any self-doubt in completing the mission. At least my body is warming. As I stare at the flames, I see myself killing E191 for everything he has done. I am not sure how I am going to do it, but I am going to get him back by taking his life. In the corner of the cave I see two bodies. For a moment, I believe that they are here to keep me company, but they are frozen corpses. I can't allow my fate to become like those people. I approach the frozen corpses and see they are holding hands. Their bodies are perfectly preserved from the ice-cold conditions.

"Did both of you give up too soon? What mission were both of you on?" I know they won't speak back. I sit in front of the fire again and stare at the crackling embers. I lift my battle suit and see a symbol on my solar plexus that drew itself after I found the first key. How is that possible?

The following morning as the sunlight hits the cave's entrance, I wake up to a fireless pit. The blizzard has passed. Now I am hungry. I have eaten all my rations, and now I must hunt for food. But what life can survive here on this icy continent? I leave more footprints in the snow while looking for any animal to kill. My stomach growls, not a bird in the sky or small animal to catch on the ground.

I reach a large body of water with ice platforms on the surface. My body is picking up strong electromagnetic signals from the other side of the freezing water. The next key must be there. This is going to be risky, but I have no other options. It's either standing here freezing and starving to death or finding a way across.

I hop from one piece of floating ice to the next,

staying focused on the frozen shelf of ice in the distance. As I get closer, I see glowing spheres in the snowy-white void. I am only a few jumps away. On my next jump, I think I landed securely on the ice platform, but my foot slips and I plunge into the freezing water. I was so close.

The water is so cold that every muscle in my body tenses up and locks in place. I must be going into shock. I want to swim out of the cold water, but my body won't allow me to move. A few codex hands reach down to pull me out. I come back to my senses. A group of codexes wearing animal furs sit me up and smother me in blankets.

"I have never seen a human with codex augmentation," a codex says. "This is fascinating."

Another says, "Harold, she is hypothermic. Her heart can shut down at any moment. Let's focus on getting her back to the igloos to stabilize her."

That is interesting. They refer to each other using human names. They take me to a giant camp of igloos that has advanced technology supporting the ice shelters. The technology attached to the massive igloos must keep the ice in a permanent frozen state. More codexes come out from their homes, curious of the foreigner on their icy land.

My body finally stops shaking. I address the codexes. "My name is Lucy from the continent of

Atlandia. The last continent on the planet that has thriving human civilizations trying to rebuild the utopias of the past. But now my country is in peril. War and illness will spread from my home to the rest of the world if I don't successfully complete my mission. On this continent is a key that I need to find. I need to find the key before E191 does. He is a codex from the era of the old ways. He once tried to overthrow Paradise but failed. He's back and stronger than ever."

A nomadic codex steps forward. "Did you say E191?"

Another says, "Yes. The human female did. This can't be true."

They come to me and show me their shoulders. It's a faded design of a logo that illustrates fire.

"We used to be in the rebel militia to overthrow the overseer. Most of the rebel army was terminated when the overseer revealed a trump card we didn't see coming. Upgraded knights. Some of us hid away until it was all over. The regret and shame we lived with was heavy. But then Aelius freed us all and we began to think freely again."

"Lucy, E191 is very dangerous and skilled. As I'm sure you know by now, if he has a chance to accomplish his mission, he will not stop. The fact that he has returned means you must find your next item sooner than later."

I say, "I am the same. I will stop at nothing until I complete my mission, too."

A codex unit runs to me and holds my mechanical arm with both her hands. "My name is Jasmine. It is a pleasure to meet you, Lucy. On behalf of the arctic nomad tribe we will help you. First I want to show you my igloo."

I read in literature that humans called Eskimos would make igloos to survive the harsh winter elements. This tribe takes that to a whole new level of sophistication. Jasmine guides me away from the group of nomads and former original rebel soldiers to an igloo that has wiring and nanomachines at work to keep it in one piece.

"Jasmine. How did you get to this continent?"

"After our kind was freed from the grip of the overseer at Paradise, a group of us wanted to start a new codex civilization on our own terms. We all built a big enough boat from the remains of Paradise and crossed the seas until we came to Frost Oceanic. Although the conditions could not sustain much biological life, we found a way to make the most of this untouched land."

Jasmine takes my hand, and we leave the igloo and go to a remote area where there is nothing but white snow everywhere. She takes out a device, and when she presses the button, a rumbling happens. The ice opens in different spots that lead to underground caves. She pulls me by the arm, and we run down into the caves. In these caves are more nomadic tribes mining usable coal, precious metals and onyx. There are tracks where carts wheel the resources to the icy surface. She tells me that they can convert these rare minerals to power cells and create new technology. Jasmine hands me a black onyx rock.

"Jasmine, what is this?"

"This rock has been around since the prehistoric age. Some say this mineral landed on the planet from the creator of man. It's called onyxite. I believe the skytower where the false god once dwelled was made of onyxite, but it turned to dust when Aelius freed our kind. All of it was harvested in the sandy wasteland to build the skytower, but we found more of it on this untouched continent. We want to turn Frost Oceanic into a thriving codex civilization."

"My home called Atlandia has started that process to bring back the utopias of the past. E191 wants to ruin that."

Jasmine gives me a fur coat to put on that has their nomadic tribal symbol on it, which is a pattern of snowflakes.

Back at the igloo camp, I explain to the arctic nomads that I have this power to detect the next key based on these fluctuations in energy vibrations in my body. They all trust my words and gather snowmobiles they engineered on their own to help me complete my mission. I don't want what happened to the Rainforest clan to happen to these snow tribes. I need to find the artifact and hurry out of here. Four snowmobiles come our way operated by codex units. I hop on the back of the lead snowmobile, and we drive off while giving my driver directions based on the detection system in my body.

We reach a giant ice wall that stretches to our left and right seemingly infinitely. This ice wall is so high we can't see the top of it. The codexes tell me that they never bothered to scale or go around this wall. The ice wall marks as far as they can go.

We get off the snow vehicles and stare up at the wall. I close my eyes and think back to a time where me and Aelius were sitting on top of a house at Old Haven. We made paper planes to see how far we could throw them. I told Aelius how cool it is that he has powers. He told me that every living thing can be as special as we want to be. Then I remember taking the photo from Aelius again and seeing a blue light transfer into me.

I place both my hands on the ice wall, and it trembles. The ice wall opens just enough for us to drive through it. The nomad codexes try to come up with logical reasons for what just happened. They all run to me, asking questions about how I did that. There is no time to sit here and try to explain the unexplainable. I am still processing why I felt led to do what is not fathomable. Aelius must have passed down more than I can understand when giving me the photograph. We drive through the split ice wall and get to a snowy mountain.

I tell the codexes that they don't have to risk their lives to climb to the top of the mountain with me. That won't be fair to them and their tribe. They did enough to get me here. But they refuse and say they will do everything they can to get me to the top. After seeing what happened at the ice wall, they are betting their future on me.

One of the nomads tells us to get together and prays for our voyage up to the top. We hold hands in a circle. The codex prays that the creator of man will guide us on our journey and make everything go exactly the way it's supposed to go for the mission.

"What made you want to pray to God?" I ask him. "I didn't think of doing that."

"Based on everything you told us, captain. We are going to need the help from the architect of man."

"And this." I show him a tracker. "In case we get lost, we can find our way back here. I left the transmitter in the igloo."

We begin our climb, and the higher we get the more treacherous the conditions become as we traverse over slippery, jagged rocks. One wrong move and there is a death sentence at the bottom. Luckily for me, these nomads are able to calculate which moves are best to make while climbing.

After a few hours, we reach the top where the next key awaits. I don't see anything up here, yet my bodily vibrations are intense. The peak of the mountain is freezing, and the oxygen levels are so low my suit is glitching. Even the codexes are having a hard time staying online. One of the codexes trips and falls. We all help him up, and glints of bronze show through the snow. I wipe snow off an armored uniform from ancient human times. I put on the helmet, shoulder plates, and hold the sword. While wearing the armor, I remember dressing up in an outfit like this as a child. I close my eyes and raise the sword like I did in the memory I'm visualizing in my mind.

My father says, "Look at you, Lucy. You are our knight in shining armor."

"I am the brave warrior here to protect my castle." I run out of the house to my mother who is planting flowers in the garden.

She smiles at me. "My strong knight, will you protect your queen and king?"

I raise my sword forward. "I will be the strongest fighter ever."

I repeat that in real time, holding the sword forward, trying to see my parents' faces. The feeling of heat occurs again on my solar plexus. I take off the armor and set it back in the snow. I have experienced the second key.

The mountain shakes violently. One of the codexes says it's an avalanche. They all gather around me and act as armor to protect me from the impact.

The shaking causes us to slide down the mountain as they hold onto me. A massive amount of snow and ice accelerates our fall. We plow to the bottom. Heavy snow and ice bury us. I dig through a few feet of snow to the surface. The only reason I survived the avalanche is because they shielded me the entire way down.

I dig out all the codex units and drag each one to the snowmobiles. My body is starting to shake, as saving the codexes took every ounce of muscle strength I had. I secure the delirious codexes to each snowmobile and tell them to hold on a little longer. Cold and exhausted, I connect the snowmobiles together and drive the front snowmobile back in the direction we came by using the tracker I left behind.

When we get back to the village, Jasmine and the other codexes take their loved ones to different igloos to fix them. Thankfully they have the tools for the job. I wait around until I get confirmation that all of them will be okay. Seems that prayer we said was enough to get us all back alive. I wonder how many more prayers like that will work. Or did we get lucky? I can't rely on luck, or God, for the rest of the mission. God is up there, and I'm down here, trying to survive so I can save Atlandia.

As a parting gift, I give Jasmine the seashell necklace the kids made for me back home. Before leaving, I show all the codexes how to have a proper and fun snowball fight. Snowballs fly across the igloo town while we laugh and have fun.

After the snowball fight, I wave goodbye, and use their snowmobile to ride back to my aircraft with some supplies to fix the tail that was struck by lightning. I patch up my plane using the nano tech and onyx as a sealing agent. When I'm done, I leave the tools on the snowmobile, along with an extra tracker so they can find their way here to retrieve everything.

I take off from the icy continent and put my plane on autopilot toward the next destination. I lean my seat back and write everything that has happened so far in my travel journal. Debra taught me how to draw and write properly when I was a kid. This was before we had the school system we have now. I draw and write about everyone I met and my experiences and how I felt. I wrote as descriptively as possible.

During the evening, with my plane still on autopilot to conserve energy, I stare up at the night sky sprinkled with stars and hold onto the memories with my mother and father I had seen so far, thanks to the keys.

Only one more key to find. Hopefully the memory I experience with this one will finally allow me to see my parents' faces.

Early the following morning, I land my plane on the next continent where the last key is located. The moment my plane touches the ground, the temperature heats up so much I need to activate the cooling feature of my suit. I jump out of the cockpit. This place has magma pools and volcanoes everywhere. Ash floats down with a high concentration of sulfur in the air. I put on my helmet to filter the air I am breathing. Suddenly, my suit's threat detection system sounds an alert. An incredible surge of heat energy flows under me and crawls in the direction of my aircraft. I rush to the plane and grab the photograph, travel journal, and a bag of the remaining nano-technology. I jump out of the way as lava shoots out from under my aircraft and melts it completely. I watch the remains of my plane sink into the magma.

Chapter 6

I sit at the edge of a volcano and stare down at the red glow from the molten lava bubbling at the bottom. The lava is so hot that I bet my tears falling off my face evaporate before reaching the ground. Anger and sorrow boils inside me, just like the molten lava. And just like a volcano, I finally erupt and let out emotions of rage and sadness by yelling as hard as I can until my voice goes numb. I throw myself backwards onto the charred earth and watch the volcanic vapors gather in the sky.

A few birds land next to me.

"Go on, birds. You all don't need to be stranded here with me."

They don't fly away; they just stare with their heads tipping from side to side.

I swipe at them, and they fly away. I am out of rations, the cooling feature in my suit is going to run out soon, as well as my breathing filter that converts this thick sulfuric air to breathable oxygen. I am also out of ammunition and my plane is completely destroyed. I wonder what state Atlandia is in right now. Does New Haven stand fighting or has it fallen?

Everyone who I love and care for might be dead right now. I shake my head to try and get these thoughts out of my mind. If I don't figure something out right now, my home will become hellish like this place. No more thoughts about giving up and no more crying. I am Captain Lucy of the shining star that is New Haven.

I take out my combat knife and practice some striking and evading techniques Michael taught me when I was a teenager. As I make my strikes at the air, I imagine E191 in front of me with that evil grin. I swipe at the air and dodge potential patterns of attacks until I feel an intense vibration in me that makes me drop the blade. I pick up my knife and follow the energy vibrations until I come across a small group of Zeros sitting and eating. What are they doing here? I thought I was ahead of them. I need to be very calculative in my attack. There are three of them, and they are not paying attention to their surroundings.

I sneak up behind the group and sucker-punch one of them, knocking him out cold, and I take his weapon. I shoot and wound the other two. Using the pistol, I walk to each one of them and knock them out by whacking them over the head, one-by-one. The last Zero I knock out causes the gun to break.

I take one of their radios and hook it into my ear so I can hear E191 talking with the rest of his cadets.

E191 reveals his location over the radio based on longitude and latitude, so I quickly go to where he is. While doing so, I spread charcoal all over myself so I can blend in with the blackened ashy surroundings of this burnt world. I blend in perfectly with the shards of black rocks and blackened earth. With ease, I sneak past his troops patrolling the area.

I plaster myself against a slab of black rock and see E191 talking with his group. Over the radio E191 mentions how I am on this continent. E191 tells his men to scatter to look for me since his three foot-soldiers are incapacitated and aren't responding on the walkie talkie. He is now alone.

I quickly put my combat knife to his neck, and unholster his revolver, disarming him completely.

"You are very talented, Lucy. It's a shame to not have you on my side. The winning side. You really think you're going to stop me from accomplishing my goal?"

"If you make me lead commander of your army, I will join you. Plus you need me to find the last key."

I remove the blade from his neck, and after taking the bullets out, I hand him back his revolver and put the bullets in my pocket.

"You deserve to be worshipped as the god you are. You are right. There is no point in fighting. I lost everything to complete my mission. I am sorry. I understand now. My home is probably destroyed by now. Please take me in and I will take you to the tree of life."

E191 turns around and backhands me across the face, causing a tooth to fly out of my mouth. I shake off the strike and bend a knee, submitting to him. While on a knee, he whacks me over the head with his revolver. I see three E191s swaying from left to right. He picks me up by my throat, and my vision comes back.

"Master. Please forgive me for evading you this entire time. I now see your power and want to join your cause."

E191 tells me, "You really are something else, Lucy. Such a skilled soldier, but your acting needs work. You almost had me fooled at the beginning. Here is what is going to happen next."

Over the radio, he calls his squadron to return to us. His troops gather and bend their knees to E191.

"We are all going to go with you to the next key. You're going to find the key. And then after that you will guide us to the tree of life. After that, I will kill you. If you don't agree to these terms I will slowly kill you now instead."

The thing that E191 doesn't know is that I wasn't trying to act. I'm buying time for my plan to work. It's the only plan I have left with no more weapons at my disposal or transportation. If God is watching over me on this mission, I hope He knows I'm going to need another miracle.

I guide E191 to the next key, which is at the bottom of a dark pit. My energy vibrations are running rampant inside of me at the edge of this cave. One of his soldiers throws a rock into the pit, and it takes a minute before we hear the rock hit the bottom. E191 grabs my arm and thrusts me into the pit where I fall in the dark, hitting jagged rocks on the way down. I smack down at the bottom and break my ankle.

E191 shouts from above, "You know. I had a similar situation happen to me. The feeling isn't pleasant is it? I noticed you have some nano-technology with you. I suggest you find a way to use it to help you find the next key and climb out of the pit."

I sit up. Blood leaks from the side of my head. My bag of nanotechnology lies next to me. The pain from the fall is so intense that I throw up. I take the bag of nanotechnology that I have accumulated along the way and place it on my codex arm. My arm absorbs the frequency and properties from the nano tech and fuses into my body. My ankle bone heals and the bleeding from my head stops. The cave I am in shakes violently, and I hear explosions at the surface.

"Lucy," E191 shouts. "Multiple volcanoes are erupting. You better hurry up and get that key and get back to us, or we are taking our aircraft and leaving."

My heart rate increases, and I scurry around, following my internal frequency. Magma seeps through the cracks in this dark pit. I am not sure what syncing with these nanomachines did to me, but all my senses are heightened. I can see this code frequency running through every object as many colored lights. I can see the core essence of everything with these new senses. The effects from the nanomachines made of onyx from the ice lands, and the small power Aelius gave me, will not be in vain. I don't fully understand it, but it doesn't matter. I have a mission to accomplish.

I move pieces of rock out of the way and find a ring. On the ring are the words that express deep love for someone. I see memories of two people getting married, and I am their flower girl tossing rose petals everywhere. This memory is fuzzy but feels intense. I see their wedding day play out. As a flower girl, I run over to see their faces, but the experience ends and marks itself on my body again.

Lava is splashing down here in the pit. My battle suit has officially lost all power, and every system has shut off. But with the help of the nanomachines in my nervous system, and Aelius's power, I scramble out of the deep pit to the surface where many volcanoes are erupting. My plan is still going accordingly. Before converging on him, I use my battle suit's metric calculating systems to evaluate the changing environmental conditions and get a rough estimate as to when a mass number of volcanoes and magma pools will erupt to cause the most destruction. Based on my findings, we are due for one climactic eruption that will devastate a portion of the continent, and that is where E191 is leading me. The vital information I have I keep to myself, as it is the last weapon in my arsenal.

E191's team hurries over with rope to tie me up. I still hope and pray this plan works, but I need to buy more time, so I fall on purpose. E191 storms up, yanks me off the ground, and demands I keep marching. I fall down a few more times and take a few kicks to my body to force me up to keep walking. While walking, I keep the calculations and timing count in my head while I manage to loosen the rope around my wrists. It is a good thing I took the extra time training to learn how to tie all sorts of knots and how to get out of them. I am in the exact spot we need to be. But I am a few minutes early. I rush E191 and tackle him to the ground.

For the next five minutes, the rest of his soldiers try to get me off him as I remain clamped on, literally tooth and nail. They stomp on me and hit me with their guns. I can only endure this beating for so long. After what felt like a forever bashing, the rumbling from the nearby volcano causes them to stop. I jump off E191 as flames burst out of the ground around us. We duck and dodge out of the way of the lava raining down. Many of E191's rebels get hit with the lava and die instantly. This was my plan all along. My suit had just enough power to predict when and where the next eruptions would take place, and I kept those calculations in my mind.

E191 and I run to the last remaining aircraft, since the others are being swallowed by lava. He shoots at me. I take cover behind the plane. This portion of the continent is ripping itself apart. The magma flow is picking up speed, and it swallows the remainder of his rebels.

Now it's just me and E191.

"Give up or we both die here," E191 shouts.

"I choose to die with you, right here."

As soon as the thick dark sulfuric gas comes our way, I run away from the plane. E191 shoots his revolver randomly with one bullet grazing me on the cheek. I dip my codex fist into a small pool of lava, and by the flashes from his revolver, I pinpoint his location. I throw my burning hot fist into his stomach. I feel my fist go into his body. I rip my hand out, and he drops to his knees with a look of shock. There is a gaping hole in his chest. He falls over to his side, and I stand over him.

"It looks like you are going out the same way as the last time, but this time it's for good. Through fire." The blue glow leaves E191's eyes.

General Blackwater regains consciousness. "Wait. No. This can't be. This is not what E191 promised would happen."

"You chose the wrong side, General Blackwater. Your greed for power put you in this situation."

"Well, Lucy. Seems like you got what you wanted."

"No. I did not get what I wanted."

Blackwater's light leaves his eyes as some blood comes from his mouth and nose. He stops breathing.

"Now I got what I wanted," I say to his lifeless body.

The lava swallows Teddy's corpse. Suddenly my codex arm acts on its own and tries to jerk my body toward the oncoming waves of magma flow that have covered most of the surface. I hear E191's voice in my head.

"It is a good thing you have a codex augmentation I tapped into. A little bit longer, I will be able to hack into your spinal cord and central nervous system. I am going to hijack your consciousness, take my plane, and fly to the Tree of Life to become a god."

My body jerks forward toward the jet while waves of red, glowing doom slide my way. The heat is getting intense, and it becomes hard to breathe. All I can hear is E191 in my mind, telling me to give up and shoving my body to the aircraft. I feel my mind slipping away. If he gets to his plane, it's all over. I fight his control over my mind. My vision blurs. He's so close to taking me over completely. I hear Aelius's voice. And now we are in the back seat of the black van we first found when we brought him back to Old Haven for the first time. This memory is of a much younger me, but I have a mental connection with Aelius.

"Lucy, you went through all of this to find the keys. You are so close."

"I can't fight anymore. Can you just come back and save us again like you did before?"

"No. Now it's your turn to be the hero. You're so close."

I hold his hand, and my vision comes back, and I release a battle cry. Without fear of the consequences, I rip off my codex arm and throw it into the magma. I hear E191 scream until the arm has melted away. I lean my shoulder socket on a burning hot rock to cauterize it, and then I throw up from the painful shock to my body.

A piece of the continent breaks beneath my feet, and I slide downward with the plane into the ocean. I jump on top of what's left of the plane and sit on a wing, breathing heavily. The current drifts my makeshift raft away from the continent of volcanoes exploding behind me.

Chapter 7

I wake up to the sound of seagulls squawking above me, and waves roll to the shoreline of a beach where I lie. Palm trees tower over me. I turn my head.

A seagull is standing next to my face, staring at me.

I sit up and look around at the tropical environment. Bright turquoise waves rush to shore. I have no idea where I am. Did I die and go to heaven? I take a fistful of sand and let the grains sift between my fingers. I have nothing now. No plane. No weapons. No direction. No arm, again.

"Aelius, I wish you were here to give me some guidance on what to do. I am tired."

"Did you say Aelius?" A codex offers me a cut open coconut. "How did you get here?"

I gulp down coconut juice. "It is a long story. But I am on a mission that as far as I know may be over. Everyone I know might be dead right now, as I speak. How do you know of Aelius?"

"He guided me and my tribe of faithful followers out of Paradise's underground and across the wasteland."

"Who are you?"

"You can call me Codex A3D3. I used to go by Brother 01. I would preach the word of God in the streets of Paradise. Fate had brought me to Aelius. Same for you, it seems. And now here we are together on this island."

"My name is Lucy. When I was a little girl, Aelius told me a story about a group of forsaken Codex units he'd led into the wasteland to look for peace and freedom. He told me that group of codexes referred to themselves as brothers and sisters. They gave him the faith to push on to make it to the human world. Aelius was heartbroken because he had to leave you at an oasis under a tree while he pressed on to the coast. Yet, here you are, alive."

"I am alive because of my faith, Lucy. When Aelius accomplished his mission, my life was hanging on by a thread. I remember the sky flashing blue and a beam of blue light shining upward from the direction of Paradise. I knew what Aelius set out to do had come to fruition as I sat alone under that one palm tree. I dragged myself across the remainder of the wasteland because God allowed me to, and I crossed a large body of water called an ocean to get to this island. One-by-one, codexes who fled Paradise washed ashore on this island, and I took them in to start another family in remembrance of my former family whom I will never forget."

Codex A3D3 helps me up to my feet and guides me to a part of the island where there is a community of codexes wearing robes and other garments made of cloth. A3D3 tells me that there are two other sister islands nearby, that they also had made their own communities with the resources that had washed onto their shores. He tells me that every time he prays, God delivers what they need at that exact time. This community on the tropical island sustains itself using solar panels to generate power cells directly from the sunlight. There are solar panels all over the island along with lush and exotic tropical plant life.

A3D3 takes me to what he calls his personal space of prayer and peace. There are piles of books everywhere. Nothing goes to waste here, and everything is recycled. I browse through all the literature that they managed to salvage. This group of codex refers to themselves as the saved ones, and the name fits their story. It is very impressive how they managed to turn this tropical island into a home without harming the fragile ecosystem of organic life.

I hand A3D3 the photo of Aelius and his family. "I haven't let anyone touch the photo my best friend gave me, but after the experience you had with him, you deserve to have it, especially after all the good you're doing here."

A3D3 takes the photo and looks at it in silence. "God told me that I would receive an item from a human that would not only inform me, but trigger powerful emotions. You are not here by accident. The ocean currents did not randomly bring you here." He hands the photo back to me. "Lucy, tell me about your mission."

"My nation was attacked by a former Codex rebel general named E191. He made a deal with my military commander to take over his mind and body so they could both have absolute power over the world. E191 really needed a vessel to continue his mission of exterminating mankind. He sent a virus to my home and developed his former army using the Zeros who live in the wild. My country of havens got decimated. Aelius left me with some of his gift to have the ability to find these keys that will lead me to a place humans believe in. The Tree of Life. It is said that whoever eats the fruit from the tree of life will be able to have knowledge and power beyond what we can comprehend. I will use that gift to save my country."

"The Tree of Life, you say. It was the origin of man's fall from God's favor. If a Tree of Life still exists, it is not in this world anymore. It must be at a higher place. Maybe it is not an accident you ended up here."

"Why?"

A3D3 asks to see the symbols on my stomach that he saw partially from my battle suit being damaged. I show him the markings I received when I found each key.

"These are the same exact icons for the connecting transmitters we use for the cradle we built. I wonder if you are the one we can use for it. If the Tree of Life is real, we need to boost you to another plane of frequencies, if you have the transmitters and conduits synced into you."

A3D3 takes me to a boat that they made on the beach to get to their sister islands. On the sail boat, fish and other marine life swim with us and jump out of the ocean. I know there is an entire world under the waves filled with life, and that people used to study them to learn more about our planet.

After sailing for twenty minutes, the boat docks at one of the sister islands. The entire island's plant life is made of chrome. I have never seen a more sophisticated bond between technology and organic life like this before. It is perfect. It is so raw and pure I can feel the energy pulsating off the merged biodiversity and onto me as warm heat waves.

"When Paradise existed, there was a sector of solar receivers that helped power the electrical grid of the city. It looked like a floral garden but made of solar panels. It was beautiful and brilliant. I took that concept and wanted to create a new paradise, aside from what I lived in years ago. We call this sister island, Eden. Eden is a representation of what the world can be one day. Which is perfect harmony between artificial intelligence and organic life grown from the planet.

"In ancient spiritual scripture, God created the garden of Eden for mankind to exist in perfect peace and harmony with all creation. Life was meant to be perfect with the creator of man. Although this is not an exact mimic of that, one day this place can be a blessing to the world, but for now it will aid your mission, Lucy."

We get to a tall radio tower with many satellite dishes attached to it. What A3D3 did with these tropical isles over the decades is nothing short of a miracle. This radio tower is not one big receiver but a powerful magnet to draw in supplies at sea. This magnetic radio tower is the reason they are able to replenish their resources and have new codexes find this tropical paradise. This radio tower can have the power to broadcast powerful signals around the planet. They just needed a strong receiver to do so, and that is me, because of the keys. A3D3 always wanted to make a journey to meet God, the creator of man, using this tower to bring him to a higher frequency plane. But after many failed attempts, he used the tower for other good productive magnetic purposes.

The plan is to stop my heart temporarily and sync my consciousness into the powerful frequencies and energy vibrations from the intense radio waves to reach the Tree of Life. This plan is risky, but I have nothing to lose. I already risked it all to be here now.

A3D3 takes my hand and walks me over to the cradle. The cradle is a chrome solar panel in the shape of a crib that babies sleep in, and it is plugged directly into the tower. I sit on the cradle and fold a piece of paper into the shape of an airplane while all the other saved ones are getting the cradle ready to activate. I throw the paper plane, and the strong magnetic waves emitting from the radio tower keep it in the air. The airplane that never has to land. I lie down on the cradle, and codexes tape a bunch of cords onto me. I hold the photograph close to my heart. They are ready to activate the cradle and send me to the Tree of Life. This is it.

A3D3 comes to my side and holds my hand. "Have faith, Captain Lucy. We are almost there."

"How do you know?"

"I have faith."

"Then so will I." They pull a lever, and within a split second of feeling an intense shock, I am propelled out of my physical body and ascend rapidly past the sky and into the universe. I had read about outer space in old books. Mankind used to send rockets to the vacuum of space for the sake of scientific exploration. But what is farther than outer space?

All the stars, asteroids, and planets vibrate so fast they become distorted. I freefall upward into a bright blue light.

Now I am in a white void with matter coming in and out of existence. This place is amazing. All I feel is love and peace of mind. Tears fall down my face from the oversaturation of love I feel. I no longer am in a physical body. I am made up of the raw colorful energy that is creating parts of universes and life's elements, being sent outward every second. Also, life and matter that has passed its time is coming back here to be propelled upward or downward.

A giant gate made of gold and silver with a giant lock rises in front of me. The markings on my stomach float off and turn into one big key to unlock the gate. I walk through the gate, and every step I take leaves behind these vibrating pools in which I briefly experience life with my mother and father from when I was a little girl. But I still can't see how they look. A seed drops from this golden light from above and stars appear. From the seed a giant tree made of vibrating energy grows in front of me. I am having a hard time comprehending the size of this tree compared to me. This tree is the size of an entire galaxy that I traveled through to get here, and I am just a spec compared to it. There are glowing blue neon fruits that are too many to count. More than the stars in the universe.

A paper plane flies around me and lands at my feet. I pick up the paper plane and see someone standing beside me.

"Long time no see, Lucy. You have grown so much. I am glad you made it here," Aelius says to me.

I run and hold Aelius tightly. He is no longer in the likeness of A191, stripped of the codex exterior. "I missed you so much, Aelius. You always remained my best friend, and I became a strong warrior for you. Have you been watching over me?"

"I have been watching over you, Lucy. And I am very proud of what I have witnessed. It is an honor, Captain."

"Am I dead?"

"Far from it. However, I am only allowed to be here for a short time to help you accomplish your mission and save the world. Each fruit from this tree is a piece of light that came into existence when reality as we know it was first made by the creator of man, God. I am here from a place called Heaven. Lucy, this place between life and death is only a fragment of what your mind can visualize and comprehend right now. I couldn't even begin to tell you about that next step of the journey, but it's not your time to pass on yet. For now, you must take a bite of the fruit from the tree to complete your mission. Whoever is able to access this place and take the fruit will be allowed the chance to fulfill their desires for a brief moment in time. I know you may want to use the fruit to experience a life with your mother and father again, but you already know what you must do."

"As much as I want to experience a lifetime with my mom and dad, I need to complete my mission for my family in New Haven. They and the whole world are counting on me. I am so happy I got to see and speak with you again, my friend. I am a soldier and will keep fighting the good fight until the end."

Aelius points toward the tree, and a branch lowers as I walk closer to it so I can pick the glowing bright blue fruit. I hold the fruit in both hands and feel the pulsating energy flowing in and out of me. It looks to be the shape of an apple made of raw blue energy.

"Lucy, whoever takes a bite of the fruit and does what their heart desires loses their own life. But, when I gave you the photograph and transmitted some of my gift to you, that will counteract the sacrifice that's required when taking a bite from the fruit. That photo gave you the gift of direction, which is how you found the keys. Harmony, which is how you integrate so easily with advanced technology. And love, which is for this moment. Because of our stronger gift of love and friendship, we can save the world again. When you return, you will no longer have the abilities you had during your mission. But that did not make you special. Your drive to push on for love is what makes you special, and I can't wait to see how the rest of your life unfolds with the creator of mankind. Also, tell Michael and Debra I love them too, and we will all see each other when the time is right."

I hug Aelius and give him a kiss on the cheek. I take a bite of the fruit, and I explode into particles of energy and come back together again, over and over, until streams of colorful lights engulf me, and now I am one with the universe. I feel every part of the universe and everywhere at once, but present at the same time. In this state of conscious raw energy, I create a path of light back to my universe and cross the bridge made of every memory my species has ever had from the beginning until right now. At the end of the bridge, I see my home world and the virus that smothers it like a storm cloud, which I make disperse and clear. I am able, as this giant cosmic divine entity of conscious life-force, to pick apart the molecules of the virus. The country of Atlandia is now free from the plague. When I killed E191, the Zeros stopped attacking. I see all the Zeros standing down. I morph back into my body and freefall from the higher plane that exists before the mysteries of the afterlife, or heaven, and as I fall through the universe and vibrate energy signals, I hear Aelius tell me to enjoy this one final gift. I relive all the moments with my mother and father like a story book. All the family trips, birthdays, all the loving moments. And I finally see clearly how they look.

I land softly back in the cradle and sit up to see A3D3 and the other saved ones praying and kneeling beside me for a safe return. A3D3 sees me awake and runs to hug me. We hold each other firmly, and I don't want to let go. The other codex family comes over, and we embrace each other.

"Lucy, please, you have to tell us. What was it like?"

"Everyone. I honestly can't describe it in words. Every second that passes, it becomes a hazy dream. It's like a distant memory that happened lifetimes ago. Yet, it left an imprint on my heart and soul somehow. All I can say is, there is so much to life that we don't know about, but we are just scratching the surface of what else is part of existence itself. The spiritual mysteries are not mysteries, they are real. We just haven't learned to comprehend it yet."

"I always knew they were real. I can't wait to use the radio tower to explore what lies beyond the known physical universe. Some things might always be beyond human and codex comprehension, and that is a blessing, too. Let's get you back home, captain."

A3D3 makes a new and secured boat for me with enough food and water to get back to mainland Atlandia. I say my goodbyes and begin my journey back home.

Chapter 8

I lie back in the sail boat and watch the sky pass by. What an adventure this mission has been. So many times I almost failed, but the people and codexes I met along the way carried me to the finish line. The sail moves easily from the ocean breeze, guiding me gently back home. I should be at the shores of New Haven in a few hours. I write and draw in my travel journal. I sit at the edge of the boat, and with my one arm, let my hand glide on the navy-blue ocean surface. The New Haven shores appear and I stand at the front deck of the sailboat, holding the sail to balance myself the rest of the way.

I hop off the boat and plant my two feet on the beach of New Haven for the first time in a month. The beach is full of artillery rounds and ditches for trench warfare. The walls of New Haven are battered. One of the patrolmen sees me.

"Captain Lucy has returned," he shouts.

The gates open, and I take a few steps inside. Debra stands across from me with a group of soldiers pointing their guns toward the open gate. We stare at each other, and I can see in their eyes they have seen and been through a lot. Debra's straight face turns to a smile, and so does mine. We run to each other and embrace.

"I did it," I cry out in her arms. "I did it. I completed the operation."

One of the soldiers drops his weapon and runs away, shouting at the top of his lungs that the fighting is over and that I completed the mission. Other guards fall to their knees and express gratitude that the killing is over.

Debra tells me, "Your arm. Are my eyes betraying me?"

"Yeah. They got an arm. But we won the war. It's a long story."

"We were a few more hours from getting overrun completely. The virus killed more people and caused our forces to be ill. The last bit of medicine they salvaged gave them just enough strength to hold on. We were the only Haven that didn't completely fall. We stood our ground and fought for days and days. Just killing and dealing with the disease. Then suddenly, the Zeros stopped attacking, and those who were sick miraculously got better. We took advantage of the moment to strike back with everything we had. As the Zeros were defenseless, our army didn't kill them. We couldn't understand why they just stopped, but it was our moment to regain the upper hand."

"Where is Michael?" I ask.

Debra takes my hand and escorts me to where Michael is atop the southern portion of the border wall. Everyone I walk past salutes me or takes a knee. Atop the wall, TJ is with Michael but now he sits in a wheelchair. I salute TJ for taking that next step as a soldier and watching over things here. Instead of saluting me back, he gives me a hug and kiss on the cheek.

I say jokingly, "Hugs are a little harder to give with only one arm."

TJ takes a step back. "It's good to have you home, captain. We held it down here, and we were ready to go down with the ship." We salute and I walk over to Michael. We both gaze into the setting sun.

"My daughter. It's good to see you back. Thank you for all your services. I can't even imagine what the journey must have been like. Judging from the missing arm, I am sure you will have a lot to tell your command about. New Haven remains the shining star with wings."

I ask Michael, "How did you end up in this wheelchair?"

"The same way you lost your arm. Fighting for what I love. So many sacrifices were made."

The trumpets blow from down below on the streets, and other instruments are played as crowds gather at the haven's central square. The flags are raised of our New Haven symbol all along the border wall and sway with pride.

"Lucy, it's time for you to address the people," Michael tells me.

I walk into the middle of the crowd with Michael wheeling along beside me, and I take in everything around us. Most of the civilians have bandages and visible injuries. They are no longer civilians but warriors who fought with all they had for their home, too. After seeing how everyone did their part for our shining symbol of hope, I bury my face in my remaining hand.

Hannah comes up to me and puts her hand on my shoulder.

I look up and shout to everyone, "Operation Saving the Gift is successful. We won. We won." An eruption of cheers and screams of happiness fills the city, and I look up at the sky, knowing Aelius is watching all this. "The mission was a success, not because I did it all on my own, but because I had lots of help along the way. I had to travel to many continents and discovered people and codexes that live a different way of life than us. But they believed in me and the cause. The world is so much bigger than Atlandia. Without the encounters of different families and nations, I would have never made it. To everyone who is my family and all the refugees of other Havens here who lost their homes, let's use the success of this mission to be better in unity for future generations. Then this operation will truly be a success."

I walk through the crowds that are clapping for me and go to be alone at the garden where the Aelius and Joseph tribute stands. What a journey it had been. I take a long breath and feel as though I could fall asleep while sitting here on the park bench. Bullet casings are scattered about, and there are no more flowers. The experience I had at the Tree of Life is fading away like a dream. It feels like it never happened. I know it did, but my mind barely can hold onto that supernatural experience anymore. Still, I vividly remember the memories of my mom and dad.

I stand up and kiss my hand and tap the tribute statues. I go back home. There is celebration in the streets. Though I need a bath, I sit on the roof of my home and make a paper airplane. I toss it and watch it fly. I miss my real airplane.

By the next year, the rebuilding process has taken place. Teddy Blackwater went down as the greatest traitor in our era because he almost sent us back to the ways when humans were on the brink of extinction. I have been named the general of the New Haven armed forces. The railroads are restored, and all twelve Havens help each other rebuild. As for the

Zeros, we gave them a fair choice to be a productive member in society, or be kept in prison. Most of them elected to work jobs and become law-abiding citizens.

One morning I go to the beach where a group of codex engineers upgrade my new aircraft with new modifications. I use my new prosthetic arm's hand to rub the exterior of the plane. She is beautiful.

I smile at Hannah. She's a new recruit for the New Haven force, going through an early morning roll call. I am so proud of her.

I hop in my aircraft and take off from the beach and fly to Paradise, which has been turned into a museum and public historic site. It's only fitting that codex units are the tour guides to explain the history of their own kind to the upcoming generation of people who want to know about that part of history, though every part of history matters. The good and the bad. And as the two dominant species, we must record the truths of the past to help grow the future. Runways for aircraft were made for planes to land near the Paradise ruins. They come from all over Atlandia to learn about the history of codexes.

I stand where E191 and I had our first encounter. While tour guides walk all around me, I kneel, and grab a fistful of sand. If the roles were reversed and I was born into the situation E191 was in, would I have the same goal and hatred for humans? Looking back at it now, I couldn't really blame him for pursuing his mission the same way I needed to accomplish mine for my family. At the end, my will was stronger. The mission of good put down evil.

I let the sand blow out of my hands, and decades continue to pass by. The entire world is reconnecting again, and other continents build their civilizations to a similar model we do here at Atlandia. Now as an elderly woman, retired from being general of the New Haven force, the age of peace has dawned. I married and had children of my own, became a proud grandmother, too. By now Michael and Debra have passed away, and Hannah is the new leader of New Haven City, and she is now raising her own family. The utopias that man and codex once built are returning.

I turn on the television, and a news segment airs about possible space exploration being funded. The first rocket ship is now being engineered.

My grandson, Aelius Jr, runs over to sit on my lap.

"Grandma, I want to hear more about your cool stories from when you were younger and saved our civilization."

"Of course, Aelius. Go get my travel journal to help jog my memory, and I can share it with you until Mommy and Daddy get home."

Aelius Jr. jumps off my lap and sprints to get the journal and runs back to me. "Grandma, I want to be an amazing explorer like you used to be."

"You will be, Aelius. I can see the passion in you. When one adventure ends another begins, and yours will be greater than those who came before you."

I put on my reading glasses and begin to tell him about Operation Saving the Gift.

Michael Colon is a creative freelance writer and novelist, born and raised in the Big Apple, New York City. He uses his craft to profoundly impact the lives of others with thought-provoking words that breathe life into his characters. He often equates his writing to painting masterpieces with prose. His inspiration comes from various societal abnormalities, cultural differences, and his own life experiences. When he isn't writing, he enjoys working out, watching sports, visiting museums, and exploring nature trails.

More Books by Michael Colon

The Gift from Aelius

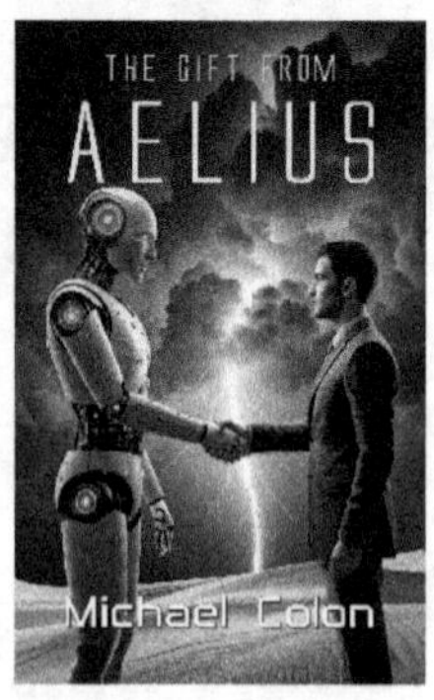

In the not-too distant future, A191, a Codex with artificial intelligence, feels like a misfit in Paradise, a walled city in the middle of an endless desert where humans imprisoned his race long ago. He's not like the others of his kind; he longs to meet humans and make peace with them so man and Codexes can be reunited in the world. These thoughts and feelings are not allowed in Paradise; he risks banishment to the desert by the Overseer A. I. who rules by fear and force. Complicating matters, A191 has a glitch in his programming that conjures up a human boy named Aelius who tells him to go to Old Haven where he will find freedom. However, he's drafted into a rebellion against the Overseer, and as Paradise enforcers close in with orders to terminate him, he escapes the city to wander the desert in search of humans. The journey reveals the truth about his existence, the Overseer's lies, and the consequences of mankind's untethered technology.

The Greatest Comic Book Tale Ever Told

Sonny Forever, a teen foster child living in the slums of Irontown City, sees no purpose in his life. He wonders why his parents abandoned him to an orphanage. Constantly battered by bullies, he has no friends and escapes into comic books where real superheroes live. He actually sees them floating in the sky and yearns to fly with them. His dreams and reality collide, as a shadow phantom appears and warns him against seeking his parents and the reason he was born. His foster mom tells him he's special, that he's a superhero in his own right, but he has to learn the truth and decides to find the old orphanage. However, the shadow phantom blurs the line between comic books and destiny, turns the page, and Sonny becomes the villain of the story who must defeat a golden glowing superhero. It's an epic battle between good and evil that will determine the fate of every soul in Irontown.

www.ingramcontent.com/pod-product-compliance
Lightning Source LLC
LaVergne TN
LVHW020718110826
845149LV00012B/2315

* 9 7 8 1 9 6 7 8 8 8 1 2 2 *